THE SECRET OF CASTLE BALOU

by

Janet Rogers Howe

Illustrated by H. Tom Hall

"A dungeon! Did you hear that, Sheba? Paolo said there's an old dungeon here in the castle!" Jonathan was excitedly talking to his dog. He had come to spend the summer in a castle over 500 years old, north of Rome, with his aunt and cousin. Jonathan found that another boy, Paolo Rossi, was there visiting his uncle, and his dog, Balou, was always with him. The boys planned to explore the dungeons for a treasure said to have been left by the Germans during the war. Jonathan wasn't happy about his cousin, Leila's, arrival, because she was smart and might spoil their plans, so they tried to keep them a secret from her. Leila had some plans of her own, though, and made some interesting discoveries. Jonathan got trapped in the old dungeon, but the two boys' dogs helped solve the secret of the ancient castle.

* * * *

Classification and Dewey Decimal: Fiction (Fic)

About the Author:

JANET ROGERS HOWE has an absorbing interest in dogs and horses and a rare insight into the interests and activities of young people. Mrs. Howe devotes most of her day to writing.

About the Illustrator:

H. TOM HALL, a native of Pennsylvania, attended the Tyler School of Fine Art of Temple University and graduated from the Philadelphia Museum College of Art. Mr. Hall spent two years in Japan while serving with the United States Army. With his wife and sons he lives in the farm country of Pennsylvania.

THE SECRET OF CASTLE BALOU

THE *Secret*
OF
Castle Balou

by

JANET ROGERS HOWE

Illustrated by H. TOM HALL

1967 FIRST CADMUS EDITION
THIS SPECIAL EDITION IS PUBLISHED BY ARRANGEMENT WITH
THE PUBLISHERS OF THE REGULAR EDITION
THE WESTMINSTER PRESS

BY

E. M. HALE AND COMPANY
EAU CLAIRE, WISCONSIN

To our kindly castello friends,
Maria and Vittorio

Contents

1

ⅢⅢⅢ

The Room in the Tower

A s THE official United States Army car moved onto the level open space on the winding hill road to Castle Balou, young Jonathan Swift leaned far out of the open window. He gave such a wriggle that Sheba, the brindle bulldog, on the seat beside him woke up with a grunt of protest.

"Hey, Ryan, I see a boy and a big white dog on top of one of the towers. I think they're watching for us." Jon cupped his hands around his mouth and shouted a lusty *"Ciao!"* and then waved frantically. The boy waved back.

Corporal Ryan slowed the car to a crawl. "Look, Jon, the Colonel commissioned me to get you and that bulldog of yours here in one piece," he cautioned. "Take it easy. We'll be there in another couple of hairpin curves, I hope."

Jon settled back on the seat, feeling happier. This brief but unexpected exchange had bolstered his spirits. The plan for him to spend the summer with his aunt and young cousin several hundred miles north of Rome had been made overnight. He hadn't yet recovered from the speed with which it had come about.

11

He knew he should be used to the sudden secret missions his father often had to make. But having to spend a whole summer with Aunt Agnes, his father's bossy sister, and Leila, his own cousin, had made him want to rebel. His father's Army training didn't allow rebellion, and Jon had been feeling grim about the arrangements ever since.

He relaxed and rubbed the small, soft ears of Sheba, the English bulldog, his devoted friend and often his only confidant. "Maybe this will be a break for both of us, old girl. A boy and a dog." He tightened his arm across her heavy shoulders. "Dad didn't tell me that. Maybe this summer won't be so bad, after all."

Corporal Ryan mumbled sympathetically. "Good thing you speak Italian, Jon. Guess dog-talk's the same in any country, but human lingo sure isn't." Ryan groaned with the effort of steering the big car round another U-turn. "Whoever built this roller coaster road did not expect anything bigger or speedier than a donkey ever to use it. No wonder the place was a fortress in olden days. An army'd be worn out before it could attack."

He heaved a vast sigh of relief when he swung the car around a double turn and up a steep incline onto a level open space where the long drive ended. To the left, vine-covered stone walls rose steeply above a wide, dry moat that separated the castle-fortress from the area where the car had stopped.

"This must be it, Jon," Ryan said. "Spooky old dump, if you ask me."

Jon nodded but didn't answer. He had seen several things to interest him. First he saw his Aunt Agnes, tiny, erect, a miniature of his West Point trained father, walking toward him from a shady spot under a cluster of tall umbrella pines. He had noticed a smiling couple standing quietly near the end of the drawbridge, and over at one side, discreetly screened by a clump of box-wood, were the same boy and white dog he had seen in the tower only minutes before. He caught a quick, restless movement from them, but after a fleeting glance in their direction, Jon moved forward to greet his aunt.

"How tall you've grown!" she commented as she waited for him to lean over so she could kiss his cheek. "You're getting to look more and more like your mother. Where has your father disappeared to this time? Do you know?"

"Classified official business again, destination un-known, Aunt Agnes," he answered. He hadn't time to say any more when she saw Sheba at his heels.

"I see you've brought that snuffly bulldog with you," she said with marked disapproval. "I can only hope she'll get along with Balou, the big castle dog. He's a Great Pyrenees, and a true aristocrat. He barely toler-ates other dogs. I hope she won't stir up any trouble."

Before Jon could tell her that Sheba too was fussy about any friends she made, his aunt had already turned to introduce him to the couple he had noticed waiting near the drawbridge. They were Maria and Vittorio Rossi, who supervised the running of the castle, inside and out. They acknowledged the intro-duction with a friendly welcome, but when Jon spoke to them in their own language they glowed with pleasure.

Aunt Agnes raised her eyebrows in surprise. "Your father has had you learn Italian, has he? Of course, since you and he live in Rome, perhaps he's wise. I'm having Leila speak French. I feel that will be much more important to her socially."

Her remarks made Jon grit his teeth, but before he could think of a polite answer, Sheba moved into sight. She had noticed Balou standing half hidden, quietly watching what went on.

Sheba shook her short-legged body and moved deliberately toward him. A few feet from him she stopped and lifted her head so she could look up into his face, her eyes unblinking.

Balou stared down at her, motionless for several seconds. Then he moved forward to touch his nose to hers, and to put his right front paw gently on her solid shoulder in a majestic gesture of acceptance before he moved away.

Sheba's homely frog face looked as if she were smiling. She wriggled back to Jon, her tail wagging so hard it sent ripples under the loose skin along her spine. Jonathan felt a twinge of regret as he watched. He realized this meant that for the first time he was going to have to share her devoted affection with Balou.

He looked up to nod to the boy, but neither the boy nor Balou was in sight. When Jon saw that Corporal Ryan and the two Rossis had disappeared, he turned quickly to make sure that his aunt was still there.

"Where'd everyone go, Aunt Agnes? Is this place full of secret stairs or hidden doors?" he asked. "Where's the front door?"

"Farther on. We go through that oak door across the

drawbridge and through the rock tunnel, first. You'll
see for yourself in a minute." She added: "I'm told that
there are secret stairways and hidden passages, but
since I prefer to use the regular ones, I haven't investi-
gated. Come, Jon, I must tell Vittorio where to put
your luggage."

Sheba kept close to Jon's heels as he followed his
aunt along a long, narrow passage cut from a tremen-
dous ledge of solid rock. It was so dimly lighted and
darkly cool that Jon's vivid imagination lost no time
in thinking of things that sent goose pimples along his
arms. Unaware that there was a stairway opening cut
into the wall, Jon jumped when a hand reached out
and touched his shoulder. A soft voice spoke to him in
Italian, saying, "Take a room in the tower." That was
all, but Jon's eyes were blinking from more than the
sun when he stepped into the bright, warm courtyard
passage.

Sheba hadn't found the dark to her liking, either.
Once they were out in the open she shoved her nose
against Jon's ankle, letting him know she didn't care
for this new place. Jon bent over to give her a pat and
whisper: "Ryan was right. 'Spooky' is the word."

"Jon, the men are waiting," Aunt Agnes called as she
turned to enter another heavy oak door, which opened
into the main hall of the castle. "You arrived on such
short notice that I haven't planned what room you
should have. There are several to choose from. Perhaps
you'd like the one across the hall from the suite that
Leila and I will share."

One thing Jon knew he didn't want was a room near
Leila with her eager, inquisitive eyes. Without know-

ing what he meant by it, he found himself saying, "If there's a room in one of the towers, I'd like that."

Aunt Agnes raised her eyebrows again. "A tower room! Are you sure you know what it will be like way up there? I take it that you're not afraid of being alone, or timid about thunderstorms, or bats."

Jon swallowed as he listened to this brief but graphic list of a tower room's assets, but he was committed. Of course he had Sheba for company—but bats! "I'd like to try it, Aunt Agnes," he managed to answer more confidently than he felt.

Corporal Ryan and Vittorio picked up his things, and Jon and Sheba followed them to the door at the far end of the upstairs hall. The twenty stone steps that led to the roof were built along the outside wall. There was no roof over them and Jon could look down into the open passage below, or up to the blue sky above, as they climbed to the room. When they stepped out onto the flat roof he heard Sheba panting from the exercise. His own heart was beating fast, but Jon knew it wasn't entirely for the same reason.

Corporal Ryan peered over the parapet and whistled. "You sure you want to sleep way up here, Jon? This whole setup gives me the willies, but being on this roof takes the prize. Bats may belong here, but I wonder if you do."

Jon ventured to the wall at the edge and looked over. He was glad that Sheba couldn't join him, for she wouldn't have wasted a minute heading down the stairs.

Vittorio waited quietly, understanding what went on in Jon's mind. He said: "The stars are bright and friendly and there's a moon tonight. You can move down later, if you change your mind."

"Don't worry, this is for me," Jon assured them, forcing his voice to sound gay.

Ryan gave him another shrewd look. "I think you're nuts, plain nuts. Or maybe I'd better say 'bats' instead." He chuckled at his own mild joke and came over to shake Jon's hand. "I'd better get going, Jon. Sheba, don't you let him walk in his sleep. It's a long way down."

"Good-by, Ryan, and don't worry about us. Sheba and I'll see you in September, I hope." Jon turned to Vittorio. "I'll be down soon."

"You don't need to unpack your things," Vittorio said. "Maria will be up later and put your clothes away. Tea will be served in the drawing room in a few minutes. Mrs. Winston-Porter would like you to join her there. I'll ring the bell to let you know when it's time to come down."

Jon sat down on his bed and pulled Sheba up beside him. "Tea! I'd forgotten that Aunt Agnes always has tea at five every afternoon. Dad was right when he said she seems more English than American. He sometimes wonders if she's forgotten she was born in Boston in the good old U.S.A."

Sheba, relaxed and comfortable as she leaned against him, gave the back of his hand a moist kiss and rolled her eyes at him in affectionate agreement. Then, without any reason Jon could understand, she stiffened and gave a rumbling growl, as the short hairs along her backbone bristled.

A fresh batch of gooseflesh broke out on Jon's arms. He spoke nervously. "What's up, Sheba? You're not going to make scare cats out of us both, are you?"

Sheba answered with another growl, this one longer and louder. She scrambled awkwardly off the bed and made a beeline for the door, which opened onto the roof. Jon followed. As he stuck his head out, he heard a chirping whistle, then a hissing, "Psssst."

From behind a tangle of ancient wisteria vines that covered one of the old chimneys, he caught sight of a dark curly head and close to it the white head of Balou. Jon smiled with relief and went toward the visitors, only a few steps behind Sheba.

"Is there anyone up here now?" the boy called softly, in Italian. Jon shook his head, and the boy and Balou together slid cautiously out of an opening onto the roof. "Hello, Jon. I'm Paolo Rossi, Vittorio's nephew. I'm glad you've come. I'm hoping we can have some fun together while you're here."

Jon held out his hand to shake Paolo's when he noticed for the first time that Paolo's left arm was in a sling. "What happened? You break your arm?"

"The second day I was here," Paolo explained, "I was climbing around hunting for one of the secret entrances when I slipped and broke my wrist. It doesn't hurt much and I don't mind. I'm not going to have to do any heavy work in the garden or the fields with my Cousin Nino. My uncle says I'll have to run errands and help that way, but I don't care. The only trouble is he says I can't go poking around under the castle alone again."

"So?" Jon prompted, intrigued with his new friend.

"So, with you here, we can do it together. You'd like to explore, wouldn't you, Jon?"

Jon answered yes before he had gathered his wits to ask questions. He had barely asked, "Explore what?" when he heard the clamor of the bell.

Instantly Paolo and Balou turned away. They were about to disappear behind the vines again when Paolo called, and Jon thought he heard him say, "First I'd like to find the secret passage that leads into the old dungeon."

2

Plans Ahead

"A DUNGEON! Did you hear that, Sheba? Paolo said there's an old dungeon here." A hopeful thrill of excitement made Jon's blue eyes sparkle as he hustled down to join his aunt.

When she had poured his tea she said: "Maria has made a special cake for you, Jonathan. No doubt she'll want to spoil you the way she does their young nephew, Paolo Rossi. He's the boy you saw with Balou, the castle dog." Aunt Agnes sounded disapproving as she went on. "I suspect he's a wild young boy. At least I'm sure he doesn't have much common sense. He broke his wrist the second day he was here because he was poking around under the castle, where he certainly didn't belong."

"But, Aunt Agnes, he looked about my age," Jon said. "I'd like to be friendly with him, at least until Leila comes."

Aunt Agnes didn't answer quickly. "I'd prefer that you didn't get too friendly with him, Jonathan."

Now that he had won his point, at least enough to make his conscience clear, Jon decided to change the subject. "Is Castle Balou very old, Aunt Agnes?" he asked.

21

"The renting agent claims it's nearly five hundred years old. He said it was built as a fortress first, in the days when Italy was overrun with feudal warlords. It has been made into a livable castle only this past century."

She sensed that Jon wanted to ask many questions, so she said quickly: "I don't know much more to tell you about it, Jonathan, and I'm too busy to be interested. I came here for quiet and privacy to finish assembling your Uncle Cedric's papers before they're due at the publishers this fall. When Amy Bond, my secretary, brings Leila over, we'll be busy most of the time." Jon saw a warm smile light her face. "Having you here is going to work out well, after all. It will help to keep Leila happy. She does enjoy being with you."

Jon squirmed. How well he remembered Leila's persistent interest in him and all his activities! She tried to tag after him every second, and asked so many questions she was worse than a nagging mosquito.

Of course he hadn't seen her for two years and he wondered if she still would tell tales about him if he tried to slip away from her. It was a lucky break that she couldn't speak Italian. Perhaps he and Paolo could make plans that she couldn't understand, and they could skip off without her. That would probably be the only way they could have any fun exploring. Leila would be sure to tattle if she knew.

Aunt Agnes chatted, and Jon managed to stir four spoonfuls of sugar into his tea and eat three hunks of cake without a frown from her. He even slipped an occasional crumb to the watchful Sheba.

He was relieved when his aunt suggested he make a tour of the castle. "I don't mean scuttling around below, either. There's plenty to see aboveground. Up on the south side of the roof you'll find trees and flower gardens. The agent told me some fantastic tale about the early prisoners carrying enough earth to the top to protect the great water cisterns from cannon-balls and to grow food for the garrison too. You can see for yourself." She waved her hand in dismissal. "Dinner is at eight."

Sheba padded patiently after Jon as they climbed, peered, and explored for over an hour. They finally ended back in the tower room, where he found that Maria had unpacked and put his things away. He sprawled lazily across his bed, and when he pulled Sheba up beside him, she tucked herself close to his ribs.

"Sheba, how many different stairs did we climb up and down? I'm beginning to wonder how poor Leila's ever going to find us if we want to keep out of her sight. Funny thing, if you stop to think of it, that with all those stairs we traipsed over, we never did find the ones into the tunnel where Paolo was hiding. We didn't catch a glimpse of him or Balou, either. Wonder how we'll get in touch with them again. Aunt Agnes will never approve of our going into the kitchen to look for them." Sheba had no answer.

Dinner had almost ended when Balou's deep bark sounded from the terrace outside. Sheba, lying dis-creetly under the window in the far corner of the big dining room, moved a little, uneasily. Jon wanted to move too. In fact, he had trouble not asking if he could be excused. That would never do, he realized. He hoped that with any luck he would be able to send Paolo a message by Vittorio.

It didn't work out that way, and ten o'clock came without any word from Paolo. When Aunt Agnes suggested it was time to go up, Jon took Sheba outside for a few minutes. Even with a quick look around, they couldn't find a sign of their friends.

Jon and Sheba followed Aunt Agnes as she went up the wide flight of stairs to the upper hall where Vittorio waited with a light. "Please excuse me from seeing you all the way to the roof, Jonathan. Vittorio will go up with you instead. There's running water up there, but there isn't any electricity. He'll leave this big electric lantern with you." She opened the door to her suite of rooms and added: "Sleep well up there under the stars. Breakfast will be at eight." The door closed with definite finality behind her.

Jon almost choked on his "good night," but he turned to follow Vittorio out onto the open stairs at the far end of the hall. Sheba followed him with clear reluctance, and stood at his side when he looked up at the sky above. Somehow the stars did look clear and close and reassuring, and so did the slice of moon. "Come on, Sheba, don't chicken out," he whispered, hoping that at least for this first night no bats would be around to swoop at his head.

Vittorio hung the electric lantern on a bracket near the bed and lighted the candles in the two hurricane lamps on the table. "Maria's brought up this bowl of fruit and put a tin of sweet biscuits here in case you're hungry." Then he pointed to a blanket folded neatly

on the marble floor in the corner. "This is Sheba's bed. I hope everything's all right, Jonathan. Do you think you and Sheba will be comfortable?"

Jon assured him they would be, but he could tell by Sheba's uneasy meanderings she didn't agree. When Vittorio disappeared, Jon began to feel uneasy too. "We might as well be on top of Mount Ararat or some other desolate place," he muttered. Sheba stuck to him like glue, apparently hoping things would be better if she was patient.

He was bending over to untie his shoelaces when Sheba growled. Once again he saw the hair rise on her shoulders and backbone. This time she moved to look up at one of the windows. Jon looked in time to see something flash crazily past the outside of the window, then dart back. It made a queer squeak as it flew past.

"Bats! Aunt Agnes meant it. There are bats here, no fooling," Jon croaked with a hoarse whisper. "What'll we do if one gets in here with us? What's the matter with me, Sheba? I'm acting almost as nervous as you are." In spite of the shiver that made him laugh uneasily, Jon found enough courage to go to the window and inspect the screen. "M'mmm. It's awfully loose. I hope it'll stay in."

He had turned to the table and fished out a cookie for Sheba and selected a handful of red cherries for himself when they heard a noise. Close by came the chirping whistle that Paolo had used as a signal that afternoon. Before Jon could reach the door to open it, he heard the scratch of a dog's claws and a firm knock.

"*Avanti!*" he called, relieved to see Paolo and Balou slip in and the door close behind them.

While Paolo helped himself to some cherries, Sheba and Balou settled down on the floor companionably, watching the boys. Paolo went to the window and slid out the screen. Jon, forgetting his earlier misgivings, stood at his side, and looked out at the stars. They didn't speak as they leaned forward to toss the cherry pits into the darkness below.

When the last pit had joined the first, Paolo slid the screen back in place and said in English, "Good, weren't they?"

"Why, Paolo, you can speak English!" Jon exclaimed.

"Only *un poco*," he answered. His eyes crinkled with laughter as he added, in Italian: "But I can understand it. Sometimes that's helpful too, especially when people don't know it."

"Helpful! It's going to save our lives when my Cousin Leila arrives," Jon told him gleefully. "It'll slay her."

At this Paolo shook his head, spreading his hands out in a gesture that indicated he didn't understand what Jon had said. English was one thing, but American slang was beyond him.

Jon explained. "That's slang, Paolo, and doesn't mean what you think. You see, two summers ago I stayed in England for a month visiting Aunt Agnes, and Leila nearly drove me crazy. I couldn't move without her tagging after me. If I managed to get away, she'd run to my aunt and tattle. I thought she was an awful brat." Jon added, "Of course she's two years older now, but I'm not sure whether she'll be better or worse."

"How do we 'slay' her, Jon?" Paolo asked. "How'll my understanding English do that? Even though the castle's big, it won't take her long to find her way around here too."

"We'll figure out what to do with your English later," replied Jon. "Right now I want to know what you meant about a dungeon here. Is there a real dungeon where they used to put prisoners?"

Paolo nodded emphatically. "You'd have called them that if you had been a prisoner shut up in one. My uncle told me there used to be others."

"Used to be?" Jon asked. "Where'd they go?"

"Perhaps we'll find out about them before the summer's over. The one that's still here is easy to reach through the old wine cellar, although the secret passage I wanted to find is covered up." He added, "Because of the earthquake and bombings."

"Tell me more," Jon demanded, intrigued with the idea of more than one dungeon under the castle. "If the dungeons have disappeared, why is the castle still standing?"

Paolo explained. "The fortress was built on or out of solid rock and the walls are fifteen feet thick. The underground places were only dug out of plain dirt. There was a bad earthquake that must have loosened the dirt, and the bombings during the war shook everything until many of the underground passages were closed off by debris."

"I should think it's sort of wasting our time to explore if everything's filled up. Isn't there any place left where there's a chance to find something really interesting? Not just piles of rock and stones?" Jon asked hopefully.

"Well, there's supposed to be a secret passage somewhere on the grounds where the Germans hid the loot they'd taken."

"Loot!"

Paolo nodded, smiling at Jon's reaction. "We'll meet you up here right after breakfast as soon as it's safe."

"Safe?" questioned Jon.

"When the coast is clear and no one will ask us where we're going or what we plan to do." Paolo winked. "That's the reason I wanted to have you up here in the tower room. *Buona notte.*" Quietly he opened the door and listened intently. Then he and Balou slipped out and were gone.

Jon sat with an arm around Sheba, pondering the things Paolo had told him. When a giant yawn roused him, he said, "Must be past our bedtime."

As he drew the blankets under his chin, he murmured: "It's exciting to talk about hidden dungeons and secret passages and hidden loot. Real loot—that's even better. We never thought we'd be spending the summer in a castle with a secret, did we, Sheba?"

3

ⅠⅠⅠⅠⅠ

An Omen?

THE CLAMOR of the bell awoke Jonathan. With a
bound he was out of bed. He gave Sheba a poke
with his bare toes. "Wake up, you sleepyhead. Breakfast's in ten minutes."

He hummed happily as he showered and dressed.
Sheba, though she kept an eye on him, didn't budge
from her comfortable bed. She waited until she saw
him slick back his hair, always the final touch before
he was ready to leave his room. Then, with amazing
speed, she slid to stand in front of the door, waiting
with an air of such impatience that Jon laughed.

"You old fraud. You can fool most people most of
the time, but you can't fool me—often." He gave her
a friendly whack on her sturdy rump. "Down we go."

They arrived in the lower hall as Aunt Agnes appeared. "Good morning, Jonathan. You look well. The
tower room must have been restful, after all. We're
breakfasting out on the terrace. It's quite lovely there."

As Jon looked at the view in the clear morning air,
he agreed with her. "That can't possibly be snow in
those mountains, can it, Aunt Agnes?" he asked.

"No, not snow. It's marble. Those are the famous
Carrara marble mountains. Michelangelo went into

30

them to select the marble for some of his masterpieces. When Leila arrives, Vittorio can drive you up to visit some of the quarries. They're very interesting."

Jon nodded, and wondered what he and Paolo could do together before Leila's arrival. He brightened up when his aunt said she would be busy most of the day but hoped he could entertain himself. "Perhaps that boy Paolo will show you around. I saw the white dog in the fields below. No doubt the boy's nearby."

Before Jon could speak, she added firmly: "I'm trusting you to use your good judgment about what you do. One broken bone on the place is quite enough for the summer. Now if you'll let Sheba out through the side gate for a run, we'll have breakfast."

Sheba trotted out, and immediately the prospect of this tour of investigation sent her bounding off like a puppy. She might not have enjoyed the inside of the castle, but the outside was different and held promise enough to please any normal bulldog. Shortly she picked up the scent of her new friend. With only a hasty look over her shoulder toward the side gate, Sheba lowered her massive head and followed the trail toward Balou.

Paolo saw her first. "Balou, here's Sheba, looking for you. Go give her a polite good-morning."

Balou waved his plumy tail expectantly as Sheba waddled briskly toward him. When they had exchanged the customary greetings, they walked off to enjoy the delights of the dewy grass and the smells of the early morning, ignoring Paolo.

It was minutes later when he called them to come up one of the flights of twisting stairs with him. "Sorry to spoil your fun, but we're due on the roof this morning," he told them as he led the way.

Out on the roof, where the only trail had been left by a snail and some sun-loving lizards, Sheba looked around for Jonathan. She left Balou and trotted across to sniff at the threshold of the tower room, and bark hopefully. When there was no response, she rejoined the two sitting nearby.

It wasn't long before she heard footsteps on the stairs outside, and her ears twitched expectantly as she listened. She wriggled with pleasure when she saw Jon step onto the roof.

"*Buon giorno,*" Paolo called. "We thought you'd never finish your breakfast."

Jon looked down at the trio, a little resentful to find Sheba up here sitting with the others, her face amiable with pleasure. He shook his finger at her and said: "So that's where you went. I've whistled and called, but no Sheba. I suppose you've all been busy planning our day without waiting for me."

Paolo told him he had guessed right. "Now we're going to have a new problem, Jon. If we're going to keep some of the things we want to do from your aunt and my uncle, what'll we do about the dogs? One along is bad enough, but with two everybody'll know where we are every second."

Jon's forehead wrinkled thoughtfully. "All I can say is that if Sheba's going to desert me for Balou, we'd better start with him. Does he always keep so close to you? After all, he's not your dog. Why's he your shadow like Sheba's mine?"

Paolo looked shy as he ran his hand over Balou's thick coat. He said proudly: "We're like brothers. To go back years and years ago, the first pair of Great Pyrenees was given to the lord of this fortress in payment of tribute. They belonged to a Spanish silk merchant he'd taken into custody. Since then there's always been a Great Pyrenees here named for the castle, but this Balou is the last."

At his name Balou looked into Paolo's face and edged closer to him. Paolo said quietly: "You see I was only seven when I came here the first time and I'd just lost my mother. Balou was a puppy, and he'd lost his mother, too. We comforted each other then, and ever since we've been like brothers whenever I'm here."

Remembering his own loneliness, Jon found he had a lump in his throat. "I know what you mean because it was when I lost my mother three years ago that Dad gave me Sheba. She's a real companion and I talk to her so much she sometimes acts as though she understands what I say to her."

Embarrassed to mention anything so personal, Jon stood up and added casually: "If they're going to be a nuisance, why don't we shut them up together? They'd be company for each other. If we can't do that, maybe we can tie them up near us but out of sight."

"We don't need to worry about them today," Paolo said. "I'm going to show you around the outside so you can learn where the paths and shortcuts are. You'll see how wise the man who built this was when he planned it."

"But I thought you said you wanted to look for a secret passage into the dungeon, Paolo," Jon said, disappointed at the tame program Paolo suggested.

Reluctantly Paolo admitted: "I did. Trouble is, my uncle's too smart. He must have suspected we'd make plans to do things together. At breakfast he told me that just because you had come didn't mean I'd better take you places where you'd break any of your bones." Paolo chuckled. "He said to plan to stay outside for a while."

"But that means we can't do anything that's exciting, Paolo," Jon said. "How long does he mean by 'a while'?"

"Don't look so upset, Jon. There's a lot to see and find all around the castle. For instance, a long time ago Nino mentioned something about a concealed entrance up on the hill. I'll try to coax him to tell me about it so we can keep our eyes open for that. Nino often tells me things that my uncle won't."

As they walked through the deep moat they looked up at the slanted openings cut out of the walls. Jon asked what they were, and Paolo explained. "The soldiers used them if the enemy got over the outside walls and past the crossbows and the cannons fired from the top. They poured flaming hot oil down into the moat through these holes. That's why they're all slanted downward."

Jon was busy picturing this scene when Balou, with Sheba puffing at his side, discovered a sluggish snake sunning in the footpath ahead. Without hesitating, the dogs bravely drove it back into its den.

"Snakes too!" Jon exclaimed. "They're not poisonous, are they?"

"No, at least I never heard that they were," Paolo told him. "To hear the stories some of the village people tell, there are worse things than snakes here."

"Such as?" Jon asked, not liking the idea of snakes much better than he did bats. "What's worse?"

"Ghosts," Paolo told him in such a solemn tone of voice that Jon shivered. "The ghosts of the dead prisoners. On stormy or windy nights, they claim, you can hear them moaning way down in the village itself."

Jon muttered: "Bats, snakes, dungeons, and ghosts! This place has everything built in for a jolly Halloween party."

Paolo was pleased with Jon's reaction. "That's only at night. It's sunny now. Let's walk around the entire place and look it over. Maybe we can find some good solid ledges to climb where we can break our necks if we're not careful."

They stopped first at the neat yellow stucco barn with its red tiled roof. Inside, the freshly cut hay smelled sweet. The brown Swiss cow mooed gently when she heard them come, and in one corner a small gray donkey waggled his long ears and brayed so noisily Sheba barked.

"That's Pinocchio. He's a strong-minded little rascal, but nowadays he's lonely. He'd like to go for a walk with us because the Count's always spoiled him, letting him do most anything he wants."

Jon started to ask some questions about this Count when Vittorio called Paolo to remind him he had an errand to do in the village. Together the boys and dogs picked their way down one of the steep, narrow short-cuts.

They came back along another that led into the field at the foot of a jutting promontory of solid rock. "I'll bet no enemy ever scaled this hunk of granite," Jon commented, squinting his eye to figure the height.

"No, and we're not going to, either," Paolo said. "Let's sit here and finish the candy we bought."

While the boys ate their candy, the dogs did the exploring. To Jon's surprise, Paolo asked: "What's your cousin Leila look like? Is she pretty?"

Jon shrugged his shoulders. "I dunno. Two years ago she was little and skinny. She wore her hair pulled straight back in a ponytail, and she had freckles all over her face. I thought she was homely, and I know she was an awful pest. She was smart, too, and that made her worse." He looked sharply at Paolo and asked suspiciously: "Why'd you ask? You don't like girls, do you?"

Paolo hesitated, then answered vaguely, "Not much, but if they're pretty, they're not so bad." He sensed Jon's strong disapproval, so he began to fish for stones around the loose soil at the edge of the boulder and threw some for the dogs to chase.

Boy and dog fashion, this proved to be a diversion for the next few minutes. Sheba, too short-legged to keep up with Balou, finally came panting over to Jon's side, eager to help with the digging.

"All right, old girl, one more and that's it," he said, letting her take over to send the dirt flying in every

direction. "What'd you find now? That's not a stone."
Jon picked up the object she had dislodged and turned
it over in his hand.

"Look, Paolo. Sheba dug this up and it's certainly
not a stone. What is it?" He held a piece of metal so
badly rusted it had little shape. Together they looked
at it from every angle.

"Jon, you know what? I think that's the head of a
spear or a lance. It's probably one that broke off during a battle." A triumphant note sounded in Paolo's
voice. "You thought I've been joking about what went

on here in the old days. Now you'll believe me, won't you?"

Jon admitted that this was convincing proof. He turned the rusted metal over and over, feeling as if a piece of ancient history had come alive in his hands.

"Paolo, do you think this could be an omen?" The idea pleased him. "I'll bet it means that before the summer's over something important will show up."

Paolo's imagination quickly matched Jon's in speculating how, where, and what the possibilities might be. They sauntered back to the castle and began to make fresh plans for the days ahead.

"See you here about two," Jon called as he went in to lunch. He was nearly bursting with excitement when his aunt asked him about this morning.

"You'd never guess what we found. It was really Sheba's discovery. She dug it up. It's the head of an old, old spear, and Paolo thinks it might be two or three hundred years old. Why, Aunt Agnes, maybe it was used in a battle with troops from Florence or Pisa or maybe Genoa when they tried to capture the fortress!"

Aunt Agnes smiled, trying to look sufficiently impressed to suit Jon. "Good, I knew you'd be able to keep busy. And I have news for you. This morning I had a long letter from Amy Bond. She's finished the research she's been doing for me, and since Leila's through with all the assignments required in her form, they'll fly over this week. I'm so pleased, and I know you'll be too."

Sheba came to Jon's rescue by sneezing vigorously,

which distracted their attention. It gave Jon time enough to get over the shock of this news.

His appetite had gone and the time seemed endless before he met Paolo again. His spirits were low and his feet dragged slowly. Paolo only needed to take a look to ask, "What's happened?"

"Happened? Nothing, except the news that my kid cousin'll be here any day. That's all." Jon kicked a stone out of the path, which sent the dogs off, hopeful that it meant the beginning of another game.

Paolo didn't answer for a few minutes. Then he said: "This means we'd better talk things over. Would you like to go fishing?"

Jon's spirits lifted as he said he would.

"All right, I know a place over the hills where the river makes a deep pool in the rocks. There's great fishing there, and nobody'd be around to bother us."

Jon, with a borrowed pole on his shoulder, began to feel better as he and Sheba set out with their friends. For the moment Leila was almost forgotten.

4

Leila Arrives

"IT'S LUCKY for me you're here this summer, Paolo," Jon told him as they left the castle grounds. "You're going to be a lifesaver."

Paolo laughed. "Maybe you'd better wait awhile and see what you think later."

He led the way across a rocky ravine, through the newly mowed space between the long rows of a neighboring vineyard, and up and down several steep hills before he stopped. He pointed to the right. "You can see the river and the lumber mill over there. We're going left, over this way. That's where the bend in the river forms a deep pool under the boulders at the edge."

A short walk brought them to the group of rugged boulders he had mentioned. "I'll slide our poles down from here, but we'll climb across and down ourselves. I know the way. You'll have to watch out. It's pretty steep and treacherous."

Sheba took a careful look at the situation and sat down, firmly resolved not to have any part in it. When Balou, bounding ahead like a sure-footed goat, hastened down to the shore, Sheba barked unhappily.

She looked at Jon and moaned in such distress he took pity on her.

"Relax, old girl. You aren't built for climbing. Here, I'll help you, but take it easy and don't struggle."

With complete confidence in Jon, Sheba let him ease her down each precarious step of the way. Once safely on the narrow strip of stony shore she shook herself thankfully before she joined Balou. She ventured paw-deep into the water, keeping carefully away from the froth of the current where it splashed over the rocks at the pool's edge.

Jonathan, as he guided Sheba carefully over the boulders on the downward journey, hadn't seen the sign forbidding anyone to fish posted on the pole near the top. In clear, two-inch letters were the words DIVIETO DI PESCA, and the name of the owner was backed up by the number of the law that covered the order. Jon's ignorance of the fact that they were breaking the law let him enjoy the next hour to the full.

Paolo, aware of the warning and its significance, paid no attention to it. It was his suggestion that since the fish weren't biting, Jon take a swim. He said that if Jon would give him a hand, he'd have a dip, though that was all he dared have on account of the cast on his wrist. Even Sheba found courage to join them in a short swim.

The boys sat in the sun to dry, while the dogs meandered off on their own expeditions along the shore. "We can't do this with Leila around," Jon commented regretfully. "Matter of fact, we can't climb up on high places or dig around underground. My aunt would be worried. She's awfully fussy about Leila. I'm afraid I'm probably not going to be able to do much of anything once she's here."

"There are some nice girls her age down in the village," Paolo suggested hopefully.

"What good would they be? Leila doesn't speak Italian." He perked up. "Remember we said we'd speak Italian together when we made any plans so she wouldn't catch on if she overheard us."

"And remember I'm not going to let her guess that I can speak or understand English," Paolo added. "I told you that can be useful."

"Of course I'll have to be polite and include her sometimes. Aunt Agnes would lay down the law if I didn't." Jon groaned. "Girls can be an awful nuisance any way you figure it."

When Paolo didn't make any comment, silence filled the air as each boy pursued his own thoughts. Balou and Sheba came back and roused them.

"Better get started for home, hadn't we?" Jon asked. "I'm going to have to push Sheba up all the way."

"It'll be easier going up," Paolo assured him. "Balou and I'll go first, and once Sheba's started all you'll have to do is stay behind and encourage her with a boost when she needs it."

Paolo was right. Jon found that he and Sheba could scramble up more easily than they had slithered down. He had barely reached the top when he saw the sign posted on the pole nearby.

"Hey, Paolo, did you see this sign? It means fishing's forbidden, doesn't it?"

"Sure. That's been here since last time I came," Paolo admitted. "You scared?"

"No, not scared, but we did trespass," Jon answered doubtfully. "Don't signs mean anything around here?"

"Oh, don't worry," Paolo answered him calmly. "It must be after four. We'd better hustle if you want to get back to have tea with your aunt. I've got to pick peas. My aunt figures I can do that single-handed. Besides, there's no sense in being late and having anyone ask unnecessary questions."

While his aunt poured tea she talked to Jon about the book she was putting together and about Leila's plans for the summer. "She'll probably be busy studying in the morning. She has special permission to take her final examinations here, with Amy as proctor. In the afternoon she'll want to be with you. Perhaps it would be all right if that boy Paolo showed you both around. He's been here before, so he must know all the interesting places."

She looked up as there was a knock on the door. Vittorio came into the drawing room followed by a uniformed, handsome but unsmiling policeman. Suddenly Jon's mouth felt dry and hot color flooded his face.

"I'm sorry, *Signora*, but the officer insists upon speaking to your nephew himself."

Aunt Agnes looked shocked. "Why is he here, Jonathan?" she demanded.

Although Jonathan had no trouble remembering the sign and its clear warning, he said, "I'll ask him."

He squirmed with embarrassment when the officer

informed him that the owner of the posted land had seen two boys with fishing poles and two dogs where they had no business to be. He hadn't recognized the boys from a distance but Balou was all too easily identified.

Jon was thankful that his aunt couldn't understand Italian. But he realized anyone who wasn't an idiot would know from the excited tone of the policeman's voice and the expressive gestures he made that all was not well.

Jon knew they had been caught and he did the best he could. He admitted his guilt and expressed his regret.

Vittorio stood motionless until the tirade ended. Then he said quietly: "I'm sorry, *Signora*. Our nephews went fishing in posted property. The officer says the owner won't press charges now, but he warns that another offense would bring a considerable fine."

Jon began to fidget when he saw his aunt look more and more the way his father always did when he was about to mete out punishment. He could hardly believe his ears when she said calmly: "I asked you to use good judgment, Jon. This isn't a very promising start. It's fortunate Leila will be here soon. She's been brought up to observe the law. I have your promise not to go there again, haven't I, Jonathan?" She turned to Vittorio. "Please give the officer my apologies and my assurance that it won't happen again."

Jon felt limp with relief when they were alone. Inside of his first twenty-four hours at the castle, he had managed to get in trouble. Aunt Agnes might not be so lenient another time. After dinner he tactfully played cribbage with his aunt all evening. By the time ten o'clock came and she had won the final game, he was back in her good graces.

That night Sheba and he waited for their visitors in the doorway of the tower room. Sheba caught the soft pad of their footsteps first, and hurried to meet them.

"Who'd have guessed Balou'd be the one to get us in trouble?" Paolo muttered in disgust. "We'll never get away with a thing when the dogs are tagging along."

"Well, fishing's out, at least over in that place. I had to promise my aunt," Jon told him. "What did your uncle have to say?"

"He said a fourteen-year-old boy, or even worse, two of them, should know better. If I do anything else to break the law and get into trouble, I'll have to earn every lira of the fine myself." Paolo didn't look as repentant as he might, Jon decided.

"I won't get into any trouble tomorrow picking cherries," added Paolo. "My uncle figures it'll keep me busy and he won't have to worry about me."

"Sheba and I'll be glad to help," Jon volunteered, thinking of the sweet red cherries they had eaten the night before. "No harm in sampling a few, is there? If I help, maybe you'd finish sooner and we might have time for some fun afterward. O.K.?"

Paolo agreed it was a deal. The next day they worked together. Jon climbed up on a ladder and picked from the high branches while Paolo, with his free hand, picked from the ground. He filled the flat boxes that were to go to market and dragged them into the shade.

"That's that," Jon declared in the midafternoon. "Not another cherry that's ripe. But I sure am hot." He looked at the scratches on his arms and bare legs and wiped the sweat from his hot face on the sleeve of his striped jersey. "Right now I'd sure like a dip in that pool."

"You can't have one unless you're invited. But I've got an idea. How'd you like to walk over to the Murattis' and have a quick shower in mountain water?" Paolo asked.

"I'd like it fine, but where's Murattis'?"

"It's the big farm we passed on our way to the river," Paolo explained. "The one where there were some pigs."

"Pigs? I don't remember any pigs. Besides, I'm not so keen about sharing my bath with pigs, even if the water does come out from the mountain." Jon began to laugh at the idea and Paolo joined him.

"Don't worry about that. The farm's big, and the pigs stay at the bottom of the wooded slope. The springwater runs out of a pipe in the side of the hill and the water's cold enough to make your teeth chatter if you stay in it more than a minute."

"The dogs. What'll we do with the dogs?" Jon asked practically. "We don't want them to get us in trouble again."

"When we come to the fence, we'll climb over and make them wait for us outside. We won't be gone five minutes, and they'll be all right for that long." Paolo added, "The house and barn are out of sight of where we'll be."

Paolo knew the shortcuts, and it didn't take long to find the section of the fence that Paolo claimed was closest to the spring's outlet. "See, there's not a pig anywhere. They like to stay down nearer the barn so they won't miss any food that's brought to them."

Any qualms Jon had were dispelled by Paolo's complete assurance. But Balou and Sheba weren't so pleased when they found they were to wait on the outside of the fence while their masters climbed over and left them behind. Balou's sharp bark of disapproval was joined by Sheba's wheezing whine.

Paolo went back and called, "Stay, Balou, stay." As Balou reluctantly lay down, Paolo rejoined Jon. "Even if they bark, nobody'll pay any attention. Dogs are always barking out here in the country."

They headed in a beeline toward the noise of splashing water, Jon in the lead as he caught his first glimpse of it. He had raised his arms to pull off his damp jersey when the sound of a hideous noise stopped him short. Twenty half-grown pigs all squealing in terrified excitement nearly drowned out the equally excited sound of barking.

"The pigs! There must be a million of them." Jon was horrified at the racket and what it could mean.

"Balou's opened the gate to come after us," Paolo gasped. He raced down the slope, skimming over the rough ground, and Jon bounded at his side. They didn't slow their speed when they saw the open gate swinging on its hinges. Outside the fence, twenty lively pigs and two dogs were tearing senselessly in every direction.

It would have been funny if it hadn't been such a nightmare, Jon thought fleetingly. That thought died quickly when he saw the entire Muratti family, seven strong, heading up the hill to investigate the racket.

Fortunately Paolo's whistle was shrill and clear enough to reach Balou's ears. Instantly, though with obvious reluctance, the big dog turned to join Paolo. Sheba, puffing hard, tagged after him. Once the boys ordered them to lie down, that part of the chase had ended.

It had only begun for the boys and the Muratti men. For an hour the pigs dodged and darted everywhere but through their gate. If one went in through

the gate, two seemed to come out, and off they went again.

The cast on Paolo's left wrist was a handicap, but it didn't slow down his footwork. Racing at top speed, he would twist and turn until he had cornered a pig. Then Jon closed in and made a flying tackle to hold it until one of the men came to drag it back to shut it up in its proper place.

"The gardens!" Paolo yelled. "Come, Balou, we must keep them out of the gardens."

Out of the corner of his eye Jon saw Balou and Sheba working close at Paolo's side. Skillfully they drove back any pig that threatened to enter the thriving vegetable garden.

The rescue operation had been too intense and breathless for anyone to ask or answer questions.

When the last pig grunted haplessly inside the fence once more, the senior Muratti, standing six feet tall, and broad of shoulder, fixed his eyes fiercely on the two boys and demanded an explanation.

Jon's heart, already pounding from the strenuous exercise, now began to pound with anticipation of fresh trouble. What could either he or Paolo say that would soothe the just anger of these hardworking farm folks? And, he thought unhappily, how could he and Paolo explain their present misadventure when they got home?

His eyes opened with amazement as he watched and listened to his friend apologizing humbly. Paolo turned to the grandmother, who stood straight, but little, in her black widow's clothes, at the edge of the garden. She had flapped her apron vigorously to help him, and now he smiled ingratiatingly at her. He patted Balou, and asked her if she didn't think that any dog smart enough to open a gate was even smarter to know that pigs shouldn't be allowed in her fine vegetable garden. He gave Balou a whispered command, and as the big dog came over and held out his paw, the old lady's face broke into a delighted smile.

Suddenly she began to laugh, calling to her oldest son, "Aldo, Aldo," and pointing to Balou. Aldo looked and threw back his head to roar with laughter.

"Boys are boys, always," he said in rapid dialect, clearly thinking back at some of his own escapades. He shook his finger at Paolo: "No damage, no trouble for you this time. Run along home now and don't hurry back again."

"Whew, that was fast thinking on your part," Jon

said once they were out of sight of the Muratti farm. "I'm hotter and dirtier than I've ever been in my life, but at least we're both whole. For a few minutes I thought that giant of a man would at least shake the teeth out of us."

"Or do something worse," Paolo agreed. "I hope we can get cleaned up before anyone sees us. If my face and clothes look as dirty as yours, we'll have a lot of explaining to do."

Jon suggested they walk through the moat where the shrubs would help to hide them, climb up the bank behind the castle, and if they could make the tunnel without being seen, they could go up the tunnel stairs to Jon's room. No one was around there that time of the afternoon, and they moved swiftly and silently through the moat.

"Safe this far, Sheba," Jon said as he boosted the bulldog over the edge of the bank to join the others in the open space under the umbrella pines.

"Safe from what, Jonathan?" a young voice called.

Jon gasped as he saw Leila, cool and slim in a green dress. Her blond hair curled around her face and her dimples were deep as she laughed at them. She wasn't homely anymore. She was pretty, and he realized instantly that she knew it. When he saw the twinkle in her eyes, his heart sank. She might look different, but she was going to be even harder to live with.

"My gracious, Jon, you look as though you'd spent the afternoon inside a pigpen." She flashed a glance to make sure Paolo would hear before she added deliberately: "Please don't bother to come near me. I'm not fond of you when you smell."

5

A New Look

JON KNEW his face was red. He was furious to find he was as embarrassed as Leila had meant him to be. Paolo and Balou had disappeared, but he was sure it wasn't until after Leila had spoken to him.

"Leila, you little fraud. You know I don't smell—not usually. You wanted to embarrass me in front of Paolo, didn't you?" He couldn't stay angry when Leila's eyes danced with admission. "Well, for your information, Paolo is an Italian. You'll have to talk in his own language if you want to impress him."

He might as well have talked to himself, Jon realized. Leila simply shrugged her shoulders, looked down at Sheba, and winked. Then she knelt and began to talk in some sort of gibberish which meant nothing at all to Jon. The effect on Sheba amazed him.

Wagging her short tail vigorously, Sheba came over to lap Leila's fingers and sit in front of her, gazing into her face with admiration. Or could it be adoration? Was Sheba bewitched by the first pretty girl who came along?

It was more than he could stand. "See you for tea, Leila," he said. "Come, Sheba, we'd better get cleaned up." He knew he sounded cross.

His ruffled feelings weren't soothed when Sheba hesitated before she came with him. He heard Leila giggle and he hurried out of sight, hoping she wouldn't guess how annoyed he felt.

He found Paolo, cool and refreshed from a quick shower, waiting in the airy room with Balou. "Got my cast a little damp, but I don't care. I feel wonderful."

"I don't. I feel hot, dirty, and disgusted." As Jon peeled off his jersey he grumbled: "See what I mean about Leila? She gets here before she's supposed to, catches us coming in, makes me sound as if I were always a mess, and even tries to take Sheba away from me."

Paolo took up the last complaint. "Take Sheba away from you? How?" he questioned.

"She didn't really try," Jon admitted, scowling. "I remember she has a sort of way with animals. They're apt to follow her around as if she were a kind of Pied Piper. In no time at all Sheba began to act bewitched. You'll have to be careful or she'll get Balou following her around too."

"That I can't believe." Paolo shook his head. "But, Jon, you told me she was homely. I think she's pretty, and in a year or two she'll be beautiful." He went on to say something else that indicated he already had found Leila attractive, but fortunately Jon was in the shower and didn't hear him.

Jon felt better when he was clean and cool. He laughed as he explained to Paolo: "Trouble is, one, she knows she's pretty. Two, she's smart, the way she always was, only more so. I've got a hunch you and I are going to be on our toes every minute from now on or my little Cousin Leila will get the better of us."

When Paolo didn't speak, Jon continued: "Be sure to come up tonight. It'll give us a chance to make plans about how we can be together tomorrow and what we can do. Maybe you could get Nino to tell you something he's heard about the castle in the old days."

When he and Sheba went down for tea, Jon wondered uneasily what Leila might say about their earlier meeting. He was surprised when all she said was, "Hello, Jonathan."

He felt his aunt look at him expectantly and he flushed a little as he saw Leila's upturned face. She waited for him to come over and give her a cousinly kiss on her cheek. She had won that little skirmish, but at least she hadn't tattled. He was glad that Amy Bond was there and he turned to greet her.

"Wasn't it a happy surprise that one of Leila's friends gave them a ride from Milano so they could be here a day earlier?" Aunt Agnes asked, looking pleased to have her only child with her again. "We've been talking about the summer and what good times you can have together."

"Mother says Vittorio's nephew is here and you've made friends with him. Is he fun?" Leila asked, as if she hadn't already seen Paolo.

"I think so, although he's quiet and rather shy," Jon answered casually. "It's too bad you don't know Italian so you can talk to him."

"That'll be all right. You can be the interpreter." Leila looked like the Cheshire cat, Jon thought. "It'll be good practice for you, and I won't mind what you say if I have fun."

Jon fumed, wondering whether he would be able to stand this sort of teasing double-talk all summer. It didn't help when Sheba left him to go over and curl up at Leila's feet, looking as though she belonged there. He was grateful that Leila didn't make any mention of this defection.

The minute he was free that night he hustled up to the roof, this time making sure that Sheba understood she was going with him. He didn't notice when a bat swooped down within inches of his head. Paolo and Balou were sitting in the moonlight and he and Sheba sat down beside them.

"Whew!" Jon said. "I knew it and I was right. We're going to be lucky if we can have a couple of hours together mornings without you-know-who tagging along with us."

"I've got news for you," Paolo answered cheerily. "Nino got telling about things he used to do when he was younger, before he got married. It seems that the old-timers down in the village claim there used to be an escape tunnel from the castle. There were supposed to be two openings, one down near the river and the other up on one of the hills."

Jon was disappointed and said so. "That covers an awful lot of ground, Paolo. How would we know where to look? I'd rather go down under the castle and get some idea of what it's like. It would give me an idea of what used to be there. When's that time limit of your uncle's going to be over?"

"Most any day, I guess. I'll tell my aunt that you want to see the dungeon and I'd like to show it to you. She's apt to let me do what I want and not ask questions." Paolo's even white teeth showed white in his tanned face. "Let's go up around the Madonna of the Fields shrine tomorrow and take a look. You get the best view of the castle and grounds from there."

"O.K.," Jon agreed without much enthusiasm. "Sounds to me like the old saying of 'looking for a needle in a haystack,' but at least it'll be something to do."

"But that could be where the Germans hid the loot they stole. If there is an entrance somewhere up on one of the hills and the Germans discovered it, that'd be a good place to hide stuff. It'd be dry up there and easier to move later." Paolo's eagerness began to have its effect on Jon.

"Of course they'd probably put it somewhere you wouldn't expect," Jon said. "What did they take? Does anyone know?"

"I've heard so many stories I really don't think anyone knows," Paolo admitted. "When I was little, Uncle Vittorio told me there was a chest of florins—gold pieces—found somewhere in a hidden passage. Probably tribute money taken years ago."

Jon thought of the rusted spearhead he had put on the top shelf of the bookcase in his room. What else might there be? His imagination took over. "I'll be down by the barn as soon after breakfast as I can get away. Leila will be studying, but I'd better use the tunnel stairs and go through the moat, so no one will see me."

The minute Leila and her mother went up to their suite the next morning, Jon and Sheba took action.

They were back of the barn in five minutes to meet
Paolo and Balou. Seconds later they all were on their
way toward the shrine on the hill.

The day was hot, but the breeze was exhilarating.
The swallows were out in dozens, and Jon watched
them dart low, deliberately teasing the dogs. Once,
when a series of the fast-flying birds swooped down
in single formation, Sheba sat down and waited it out.
Balou simply ignored them and their antics.

"There's the shrine, up on top of that hill," Paolo told
Jon. "The Madonna was carved by one of the local
workmen years ago after a dry spell had almost ruined
the villagers' crops. They'd had a day of prayer and
that night it rained, so this was their thank offering."

Jonathan listened to the simple story of faith and
was impressed by Paolo's belief in it. Paolo went on,
"When the air raids came the bombs blew off the top
of the shrine, but there wasn't a scratch on the Madonna." He stooped to pick a fistful of scarlet poppies
as they climbed to the shrine. "We always take her
some flowers."

Jon looked at the shrine with interest. The gray
granite shrine, roofless, housed a simple white marble
figure of the Madonna. The artist might not have
been famous, but he had made the statue look real.
The face could have been that of any woman. In one
arm was a sheaf of ripe grain. He had extended her
other arm out in a gesture of blessing toward the
countryside below. It was simple yet pleasing, and
Jon didn't find it surprising to see several bouquets of
flowers inside the shrine.

He moved around to one side to let Paolo enter and pay his personal tribute.

The boys stood for several minutes looking at the expanse of country from the hilltop. Suddenly Jon muttered a disgusted: "Oh, no! I must be seeing things." He pointed below.

Paolo followed his gesture and began to laugh. "You're seeing things, all right. What you're seeing is that rascal Pinocchio, and on his back is your studious Cousin Leila."

"Hey, Paolo, she's talking to someone. I can't see who it is, but it's someone who must live in that small house at the edge of the fields down there."

From the distance, they watched the group below. Leila, in her shorts and blouse, sat confidently on Pinocchio's gray back, her legs swinging as she talked to the man below. He was stroking the long ears of the donkey and laughing.

"Paolo, I don't think Pinocchio's got anything on but his halter. How can she make him go where she wants?" Jon asked.

"She probably can't. He always makes his own decisions. But I thought you told me she could make animals do what she wanted, didn't you?" Paolo questioned.

"Yes, I did say that, but I never saw her with a donkey before." Jon watched the scene in the valley below. "Wonder who the man is? She doesn't speak Italian, yet they look as though they're holding a real powwow."

Paolo didn't make any comments, so Jon kept chattering. "It'd be smart if we found a place where she couldn't see us. Once she discovers us, she'll be up to find out why we're here."

"It's too late. They've already spotted Balou and are looking up here." Paolo was right, Jon saw. He groaned as he saw Leila shake hands with the man and then turn Pinocchio around with a tug on one of his ears.

"Let's hide," Jon suggested, looking wildly around for a place to escape. "Oh, rats, Balou has seen Pinocchio and he and Sheba are on their way to meet them. Remember, Paolo, you don't know any English, and I'm to be the interpreter. If she says anything funny, don't you dare grin."

Paolo promised, with some misgivings. Leila was pretty and there was something about her that struck him as a possible fellow conspirator. He wished that Jon wasn't prejudiced, for there could be fun if Leila were included. Paolo sighed. He had promised, so he would have to do the best he could to please Jon.

"Balou's almost as big as Pinocchio," Jon commented as he and Paolo watched the two dogs bound down the hill to meet the little donkey. "Now what?" he murmured as Leila tugged at one of Pinocchio's ears and he came to a stop. Gracefully she slid off his back and knelt in the grass to make friends with Balou, careful not to neglect Sheba as she patted the big dog.

Both dogs sat close to her, letting her stroke their heads, and Pinocchio joined in the act by dropping his nose to rest on her shoulder.

"You wait and see what happens, Paolo. Sure, she's only been making friends with them, but Balou will probably act bewitched too." Jon saw that Paolo was beginning to wonder about that himself.

Leila hopped on Pinocchio's back again. With a dog trotting on either side, the procession climbed slowly up the hill toward the shrine. The boys waited silently, their qualms unmentioned.

"Hello, Jon. Pinocchio and I've been looking for you. That nice old man who lives in the tiny cottage down there saw Balou up here and said you were probably here too." Leila smiled expectantly as she looked at Paolo and waited for Jon to introduce them. "Aren't you going to let me meet your handsome friend, Jonathan?"

I'm paying for my deceit, Jon thought, seeing Paolo's lips twitch with suppressed laughter. Although he made the necessary translation, he nearly choked when he heard each of them deliberately say things he couldn't interpret. This plan he and Paolo had cooked up to deceive Leila was certainly loaded with dynamite. Jon knew he would have to keep his wits about him and so would Paolo.

Leila, surrounded by the animals, sat on the grassy edge of an old terrace. She picked a blade of grass and sucked the tender end for a minute as Jon and Paolo waited, uncertain what to do.

"Studying seemed dull and stupid on such a nice day. I skipped out when Mother was busy with Amy. What are you and Paolo up to? Whatever it is, let's get going," she urged.

6

Two Is Company

IT WAS up to him to break the awkward silence that followed Leila's challenge, Jon knew. It was clearly his job, since Paolo couldn't or shouldn't speak.

"We came up to see the Madonna in the shrine," he told her, realizing how unconvincing his words sounded. Quickly he shot back a question to divert her. "You were talking to someone down there. I thought you said you didn't know any Italian."

Leila smiled. "I don't, yet. That man spoke such perfect English I don't believe he's a peasant, though he lives in that wee little house. He looked and spoke like a gentleman, and I liked him." She turned to Paolo and asked him, "Who is he, Paolo?"

Paolo spread his hands out, pretending not to understand. Then he looked across at Jon with a look that warned him, Take care or she'll catch one of us.

Jon interpreted and Paolo said he could answer her question only if they would both promise to keep his answer a secret.

The suggestion of another secret piqued Jon's interest, and he saw that Leila was curious too. She made the age-old gesture of crossing her heart or hoping to die, which satisfied Paolo.

Because Jon had to interpret everything Paolo said, it took time. As the story unfolded, Jon became so interested he kept forgetting to tell Leila and she grew furious with impatience. "What did he say then, Jon?" she prompted him again and again.

Jon summed up the tale, trying to use the words that Paolo used. "But the Count does not want anyone who rents the castle in the summer to know who he is or that he's living in the cottage. He's so poor he must rent it in order to have the money to live and to keep his beloved castle. The castle and his few treasures are all he has to live for now."

The significance of this suddenly struck Jon, and before he stopped to think, he blurted out in English, "Then that treasure the Germans hid belongs to him."

Paolo kept his wits and didn't answer, but Leila pounced on the word "treasure" and demanded: "What treasure? Where's it hidden? Do either of you have any idea?"

Jon hesitated long enough to make her suspicious. She looked hard at them both. "You're looking for the hiding place. That's why you're here, isn't it?"

He shook his head, but she wasn't satisfied. "I'm positive you're up to something. All right, if you both think that two is company, I'll take the hint." She hopped on Pinocchio's back and said, "I'm going to do a little investigating myself."

"I'll be hanged," Jon muttered as he watched Pinocchio's tiny feet ambling nimbly down the hillside. Leila's back was straight, and her bare legs dangled nonchalantly. Sheba was trotting down the path too, with Balou leading the way.

Paolo grunted, muttering the Italian equivalent of Jon's brief exclamation. "Balou's as bad as Sheba. I never thought he'd desert me." His face showed so much chagrin that Jon's own sense of desertion lessened.

"I told you, but you wouldn't believe me," he reminded Paolo. "Hey, now what's she up to!"

They watched as Leila stopped Pinocchio, slid off to talk to each dog, and order them back. She waited until they obeyed before she and Pinocchio continued down the path once more.

For several minutes the boys sat nursing their wounded pride. They looked at each other and burst out laughing.

"I see what you mean, Jon," Paolo admitted. "What do we do? We're smart enough to keep ahead of her, aren't we? After all, two boys ought to be smarter than one girl, even if she is pretty."

Jon pondered over this, though he inwardly questioned Paolo's logic. "We ought to be," he admitted cautiously. "Of course we can watch what she does and where she goes, and I'll talk with her, but how can we ever guess what she'll do next? Come on, let's forget her for a while. We came up here to do some investigating. We'd better stop wasting time."

"What we're looking for is the same thing others have looked for, hundreds of times," Paolo warned Jon. "If there *is* a tunnel that has an opening up here, someone, sometime, will find it. It could be us."

They decided to investigate every square foot of the hilltop, dividing it into sections with not an inch uninspected. For the next hour they moved every rock that would budge, Jon doing the lifting or shoving, while Paolo used his free arm to help. Next they each found heavy sticks and tamped and thumped systematically, hoping they might be rewarded by a hollow sound underground.

"Listen to this, Jon," Paolo cried, "over here behind the shrine. It sounds different. I think I can hear an echo underneath."

Jon listened, his imagination making him more credulous than his good sense did. "It sounds sort of promising. You lie flat and listen with your ear to the ground, and I'll whack and pound every inch of the place around here again. If there's an echo underneath, you'll hear it."

While Paolo stretched full length on the ground, with his right ear pressed into the grass, Jon pounded vigorously with a heavy chestnut branch he had dragged over for the purpose. It was hard work, and he was out of breath in no time. He kept trying, for with each blow Paolo's answer was a flat "No."

They were so absorbed they hadn't seen the dogs move away. They both jumped when Leila called: "My, your faces are red. You look awfully silly." She was back, watching their performance.

Jon knew they must have looked ridiculous, and he heard Paolo mumble, "Tell her whatever you want, I can't think of anything to say." Suddenly he began to laugh so hard that Jon couldn't help laughing too.

When he caught his breath he said: "Guess we

must look like a pair of idiots, and it turns out we are. How'd you get along with your investigations?"

Leila came over and sat down in the grass nearby. She acted so amiable and friendly that Jon felt a little ashamed to think of their plans to keep away from her. He didn't mind when Sheba and Balou curled up in front of her.

Leila pulled up a blade of grass, and when she had sucked at its juicy end a minute, she answered: "I had another long talk with that lovely old man who owns the castle. He said his name was Mr. Rafael, and we talked about loads of things. He told me he liked animals, and I said I did too. He knows about the old days here and told me some fabulous stories."

She paused for effect, and when Jon nodded impatiently, she was satisfied. "For your information, if that silly stunt you and Paolo were doing just now meant you were hunting for anything up here near the shrine, you were wasting your time." She paused long enough to say: "Paolo looks as though he'd burst. You'd better tell him what I've just said, Jon."

Jon spoke briefly to Paolo and then waited for Leila to go on with her story. "Mr. Rafael didn't mention anything about treasure, but he said that years ago during the feudal wars some of the prisoners were supposed to have dug a long escape tunnel. No one has ever found the end of it, and no one is sure whether it went up the hill where the shrine was built or down toward the river. Fact is, I guess no one is sure it ever was there at all."

Jon took time enough to give Paolo a rough translation, aware that Leila's bright eyes were watching them closely. "Paolo said he'd heard about that."

"Well, then, what *were* you doing up here so long?" she demanded. "I don't believe either of you knows that Mr. Rafael says he thinks the most likely tale is that the outstretched hand of the Madonna is pointing toward the entrance. Why don't you go see for yourselves where that could be?"

As the boys' curiosity got the better of them they hurried into the roofless shrine and gazed down at the fields below. They were so intent on this new angle they didn't notice that Leila and her animal escort had moved away. The first thing they knew was when they heard her excited voice calling, "Come over here and see what I've found."

They looked over at the small ravine filled with ledge and broken rocks. "Hurry," she added, beckoning.

They hurried, Sheba nearly tripping Jon as she raced to meet him.

"Did you look around over here this morning?" Leila asked.

"We sure did. We turned over every stone we could move," Jon told her. "Why?"

"Didn't you see this?" Leila rolled a rough-surfaced ball over with the toe of her sneaker. "It's not made of wood and it's too heavy to be an old tennis ball. What do you think it is?"

Jon reached over and picked up the ball Leila had found. "Wow! You'd never think anything this size would be so heavy." He handed it to Paolo.

When Paolo had turned it over and hefted it, he began to jabber in Italian, his face reflecting his excitement.

"What's he saying, Jon? What does he think?" Leila demanded, catching the flame of excitement herself.

"He thinks it's a cannonball, one of the small ones. When this was a fortress, they used cannons on the roof. This must have fallen here during a battle and has been in these rocks for two or three hundred years." Jon felt a thrill as he added this proof of former battles to the spearhead he had found. "Paolo says they've found others of different sizes, from time to time."

"You must have uncovered it when you were here this morning," she said, not making any mention of their oversight. "I think I should give it to the Count, don't you? See you at lunch, Jon."

This time Balou and Sheba stayed with the boys, though all four watched Pinocchio carry Leila and her trophy down the hill.

"M'mmm, guess we're not such hot explorers," Jon said in disgust. "We turned over every stone in this ravine and didn't see that."

Paolo ran his fingers through his curly hair. "She made us look stupid, didn't she? But I'm glad she didn't, what do you say, 'rub it in'?"

As the boys took the path toward the castle once again, each was busy with his thoughts. The dogs walked at their side, content to stay with them on the homeward trip.

"You've been stewing about Leila, haven't you?" Jon asked, noticing the tiny frown between Paolo's brown eyes. "You're probably wondering how we're going to keep her from making monkeys out of us every time she shows up."

Paolo nodded. "In the old days she'd have been a good general and we'd still be the foot soldiers. What are we going to do, Jon?"

"Do some heavy thinking to figure how we can get ahead of her, that's sure." Jon began to frown himself. "There's a saying that if you let the camel get his nose in the tent, you'll soon be on the outside. Leila's not a camel, but you get the idea, don't you?"

"How about your aunt? Maybe if she's cross about Leila's skipping out this morning, she'll make her study extra tomorrow," Paolo suggested hopefully.

"Don't count on that. Leila can wind her mother around her little finger if she wants." Jon brushed a buzzing insect from his crew-cut hair, then whistled softly. "Wait, I think I've got an idea. Dad's a West Pointer, and he says that when you're in a tight spot a good offense is the best defense. We'll try that."

Paolo stooped to pick up a stone to throw for Balou before he said: "Good. We're in the tight spot, all right. What'll you do in this offense of yours?"

"We—ell, I'm not sure yet, but I'll do some heavy thinking. When I'm alone with Leila maybe I can say we've some big ideas for the summer and we had wondered whether she'd like to come with us whenever she could, to help us." Jon saw that Paolo wasn't impressed.

"I'll have to play it by ear, of course," he added.

"I hope you can sell your idea to her better than you did to me," Paolo said bluntly. "I've got to go to the doctor's this afternoon. You'll have a chance to try it out then. See you tonight."

His brave words were more easily spoken to Paolo than to Leila, Jonathan realized. At luncheon his aunt had announced Vittorio was driving her to the city where the Italian naval base kept things humming. While she did her business there, she suggested they could explore the long promenade that ran the length of the city's waterfront.

With Sheba between them, Jon and Leila sauntered along the wide, tree-sheltered sidewalk. They took time to gaze across the sparkling blue water at the assortment of cargo ships, yachts, naval vessels, and an occasional trim sailboat. They met groups of young sailors, handsome and laughing in their summer whites, who included them in their smiles.

By the time they had walked the entire length of the harbor front, they were due back to the car.

Jon realized there wasn't much time left to make his boasted "offense." As they came in sight of the car, he decided it was now or never. He drew in a deep breath and blurted, "Keep another secret, Leila?" She nodded and made the same quick gesture of crossing her heart. "Paolo and I've been hoping we could do some exploring around and under the castle this summer. We'd like to find some of the old rooms or passages people mention when they talk about the old days." Jon looked quickly at Leila, but he couldn't figure out what she was thinking. He hurried on. "How'd you like to help us?"

He saw her bounce for a step or two, the way he

remembered she used to do when she was pleased. She hadn't answered him when he heard his aunt calling them.

As they went the last few steps to the car, Leila whispered, "I'd love it if you're sure that three's not a crowd." Then she added quickly, "I've got some ideas of my own, you know."

Jon was uneasy all the way home.

7

Leila Has Ideas

JON SAT in his doorway with Sheba's head resting
on his knee. He stroked her gently and summed
up some of his thoughts for her uncritical ear. "Hard
to believe we've been here only three days, isn't it, old
girl? You and Balou and Paolo and I were all set for
a good summer, but I'm afraid things won't be the
same with Leila here."

Sheba gave such a sigh of deep contentment that
Jon shook his head. "I wish I knew what that cousin
of mine's got that makes you want to desert me."

He set her aside and stood up so he and Sheba
could greet their nightly visitors. "How's the wrist,
Paolo?" he asked when Paolo came into the room.

Paolo shrugged his shoulders. "The doctor didn't
seem very pleased. He said I'd probably be wearing
the cast most of the summer. Cheer up, it's not so bad,
Jon. It'll mean less work and more time to play. By the
way, how'd that 'offense' of yours work out with
Leila?"

"I'm not sure," Jon admitted. "She acted pleased as
Punch when I asked her, and I made her promise to
keep it all a secret. But it's what she said at the end,

72

and the way she looked when she said it, that bothers me. She told me she had a few ideas of her own."

Paolo laughed. "What did she mean by that, I wonder? I think she was only trying to tease you, Jon."

"I don't," Jon said emphatically. "Trouble is, my aunt thinks Leila's a perfect angel and she isn't. Now that she isn't a tattletale any longer, I'm not sure but what she's more of a problem. I think she's apt to cook up some schemes that'll make our hair stand on end."

"She can't do much more than we've done on our own," Paolo commented. "After all, we did get ourselves into trouble our first two days together without any help from her. If she's going to 'help' us, what's next on your plans?"

Jon stalled for time by selecting two peaches from the bowl. By the time they had eaten them and licked the juice from their fingers, he had thought of an answer. "Dad's an engineer and I've seen how he makes his plans on blueprints. How'd it be if the three of us take time to make accurate sketches, by measuring the walls and towers. We can study the measurements and figure any of the places underneath that are beyond the foundations."

Paolo was not enthusiastic. "That doesn't sound like fun to me. It sounds more like a problem we'd have in school. Sure, the idea's all right, but can't we make it more exciting while we're at it?"

"O.K. How?" Jon asked.

Paolo hesitated to admit he would like to have Leila in on the planning. He knew Jon already suspected that he like Leila.

In Genoa where he lived he played with a dozen cousins and their friends, boys and girls. He tried to sound casual as he said: "It might be a good idea if we made Leila into a scout for us. She can talk to people, like the Count, and my uncle and cousin, and because she's a girl they'll tell her loads of things they'd never tell us. Since I broke my wrist, my uncle's suspicious every time I ask a question about the castle. First thing he does is ask me what I'm up to now."

"That's smart planning, Paolo. Maybe in the old days you'd have been promoted from a foot soldier to an officer," Jon said. "Tomorrow at breakfast I'll give Leila the sign to meet us by the barn. You must do the talking, with me interpreting, of course. She'll take your stuff better than anything I might say."

"*Va bene,*" Paolo said. "See you then." He and Balou slipped out into the star-studded night and disappeared. Jon and Sheba were soon asleep.

"How long have we been waiting here?" Jon asked the next morning as he and Paolo sat on the terraced hillside of the vineyard, with the dogs nearby. "It must be nearly ten. Where do you suppose Leila is?"

"Why ask me? She's your cousin. You're the one who ought to figure that out." Paolo dismissed the subject by suggesting, "Maybe she did have to study, after all."

"Maybe, but I doubt it. Let's wait another five minutes before we get going on our own." Jon's impatience made him restless.

The dogs looked up, wagged their tails, and began to bark. The boys turned to see Leila moving quickly toward them. She had a cobweb on her blond hair and smudges on her chin, arms, and bare legs. But she also had a pleased smile on her face.

"Look who's been in the pigpen now," Jon said, lifting the thick gray silk of the cobweb from her hair. "Where *have* you been, if it isn't a state secret?"

"In the dungeon," she announced proudly. "I tried to crawl through a hole that looked like a window leading out here and nearly got stuck. The bats didn't like my being there, and I didn't care for them, either."

When Jon told Paolo, they looked at each other in amazement. "Ask her why she went there?" Paolo said.

"She said she overheard her mother telling Amy Bond that there's where you'd gotten into trouble and she was going to make it out of bounds for both of us," Jon explained. "I guess, being Leila, she probably wanted to have a look-see beforehand."

"If Mother doesn't pay too much attention, I think we could have pecks of fun poking about under there," Leila told Jon. "What sort of things have you and Paolo planned?"

Jon and Paolo took a few minutes to make sure of their plan. While Paolo settled back to listen and watch Leila's reaction, Jon unfolded their proposed plan of action.

"For the time being his uncle has declared that underneath the castle is out of bounds for Paolo. He's going to try to wheedle his aunt to let him go, but meanwhile you and I'll be the ones to do the underground scouting."

"We'd better go soon, Jon," Leila interrupted. "Mother's apt to make it out of bounds for us if or when she remembers."

"All the more reason for getting at it now, at least as a starter," Jon continued. "Paolo says that since you've already found how to get into the dungeon, we can go straight there and begin to take measurements. He'll put up a ladder near that slot you tried to crawl through. We can call back and forth, and he'll know what we're doing and tell us what to do next."

It seemed a good idea to everyone but Sheba. Entranced as she was by Balou, it was more than she could endure to watch both Jon and Leila disappear. She promptly tagged along after them, and Jon said they might as well let her come.

"How'd you get in and out of the dungeon?" he asked Leila.

"I was looking for a door I could go out to meet you without either Mother or Amy catching me. First thing I knew I almost fell down some stairs and found myself in a place as dark as your pocket. It was really sort of scary," she admitted, "especially when I knocked off a bat from the wall and it kept flying around my head like crazy."

Jon nodded, feeling his flesh creep at the thought. "Then what?" he prompted.

"Then I saw a crack of light and inched along over the bumpy dirt floor into another room. That's where I found the narrow opening I tried to climb through." Leila gave an involuntary shiver. "It must have been horrible to be a prisoner, Jon. Just the same, if we could find lights enough to take with us, I think it would be keen fun to explore every nook and cranny down there. Don't you?"

"That's exactly what we'd like to do, only we want to keep careful track of the places we explore," Jon told her. "One of the plans Paolo suggested was for you to be our scout. You can talk to different people, like his uncle or cousin and the Count. They'd never suspect that a girl would have any interest in grubbing around down under a place where there might be bats and cobwebs. Get the idea?"

Leila gave one of her hops of excitement. "That'll be fun." She clutched Jon's arm. "Here, Jon, we go this way. At least that's how I got out." She ducked around some acacia bushes and through a small arched entrance in the wall. It led down several narrow stone steps into darkness, pitch-black and eerie.

"This is spooky," Jon said, wondering if his voice sounded as queer to her as it did to him. Even Sheba's muffled breathing echoed, and he could tell from the way she kept close to him she was uneasy.

"Absolutely crawly," Leila answered, her voice sounding odd too. "As soon as your eyes get adjusted to the place, we'll get to that slot in the wall. Then we have to turn around to see the bit of light that comes through."

They had barely found the opening and called to Paolo, when he called back, his voice sounding so disappointed that even Leila suspected something had gone wrong. Jon explained that Paolo's uncle had found him on the ladder and had ordered him down.

"We'd better go back," Jon said. "We need Paolo's help, and he may need ours. Let's see if we can keep him out of any trouble with Vittorio. Come, Sheba, out we go again."

Paolo's face looked dark with disgust. "You'd think I was a baby. My uncle says that until the doctor reports that my wrist is better, I can't climb up on anything, anywhere."

The three young people and the two dogs sat in the shade of a pair of chestnut trees. No one stirred until Leila reached over and pulled up a blade of grass. Paolo and Jon looked at each other and winked. This meant that something was brewing in her mind, and they waited to hear what she would say.

"This will slow us up if we can't think around it," she commented, tugging at a fresh blade of grass. "Of course I can still do what you call my 'scouting.' Anything I find out I can report to you once a day."

She's like a commanding general, Paolo thought, as he sat back waiting for Jon to go through his pretense of translation. He was amused to see how impressed Jon was after all the fuss he had made about her. It was all right with Paolo, for he liked Leila. He certainly wasn't going to remind Jon to be careful about that camel and the tent business.

"I don't see why you two can't check on the measurements the way we planned. If I do pick up any pointers, we'll know where to start exploring."

"Us two? Where'll you be?" Jon asked her.

"This would be a good time for me to get at my studying. Then I'll be ready for my term exams when the school sends them along to Amy." She explained, almost apologetically: "It's a progressive school, so you can go ahead with your subjects if you want. That's what I did and now I'm glad. Once exams are over, I'll be free for the summer."

Jon talked with Paolo, who nodded his head and said, "*Va bene.*"

"That'll take us into July," Jon pointed out, figuring in his mind about dates.

Leila gave a bounce and cried: "Good. Let's plan a real do on the Fourth. You always have one, don't you, Jon?"

Paolo looked bewildered. "The Fourth?" he asked.

Jon explained: "It's the day our thirteen colonies signed their declaration of independence from England. It's our big national holiday and we have parades and speeches, and fireworks at night."

Paolo wanted to know why Leila, who was English, would want to celebrate that day.

When Jon repeated the question, Leila laughed. "Tell him I'm half American, the half my mother always calls the troublesome part. But I'm proud of it. I'd like awfully to go to the United States when I'm ready for college. I'd like to eat lots of hot dogs and hamburgers."

"What's she think we can do about it?" Paolo asked. "People here don't know about this 'Fourth' of yours. Everyone will think we're crazy."

Leila took another long suck on the end of the grass before she answered. "I'm not sure exactly what we can do. Ask Paolo if you can buy any crackers or fireworks in the village. We'll need plenty of them to fire from the roof and the towers. Everyone around can enjoy them too."

Paolo thought he knew where they could be bought, although he also thought there might be restrictions about them.

"Let's get them first, and worry later," Leila said glibly, waving her hand as if to brush off anything so unimportant as rules. "Tell Paolo to buy all he can get. I have five pounds that Grandfather sent me for my thirteenth birthday last month. We can spend it all if we need."

Jon let out a whistle of amazement. "You're crazy, Leila. In the first place that's too much money to blow on fireworks, and in the second place your mother would never let you."

Leila's answer was to lean forward and scratch the top of Sheba's head. "Tell your master this is the way the American half of me acts sometimes, will you, Sheba? And tell him I'll square it all with my mother." Leila scrambled to her feet, brushed off as much dirt as she could, and said: "I'll go say hello to Pinocchio and then get at my books. *Arrivederci!*"

When she was out of sight, Paolo let out a muffled "Whew" and pretended to mop his forehead.

"Leila has changed all right," Jon said. "I'm not sure but that we'd have been safer if she still tattled. If this is the way she acts when her 'American half' takes over, we'd better look out or we'll be up to our ears in trouble."

Paolo agreed. "Looks to me as if she not only had put her nose in our tent but had carried it off with her, Jon."

8

ЛЛЛЛЛ

The Fourth of July

JON CONTINUED to sit where he was, even after Paolo
and Balou left him. He frowned thoughtfully, dis-
turbed by something nibbling in the back of his mind,
yet uncertain what it might be.

He took Sheba's big head in his hands and looked
into her homely face. "What's biting me, Sheba?"
he murmured, still trying to pinpoint this nebulous
thought. She wriggled closer to him and listened, with
her head cocked to one side. "You didn't care much
for that dark dungeon, did you, old girl?"

That question unlocked the puzzle and Jon swung
around to look along the row of grapevines toward the
castle. "That's it! I'll have a look." Quickly he retraced
the path Leila had taken, as far as the acacia bushes.
Here he backed off and squinted up at the slot of window she had tried to climb through. He walked back
and forth, counting the paces he took in each direction.

"I'm right, Sheba. The place we were in is only the
first part of that dungeon. I'm going to get my flashlight and take a good look down there. I'm pretty sure
that some of the places that are supposed to be under
the castle run beyond the foundations and under this
whole hill."

83

This possibility pleased Jon so much he forgot about the plans Paolo, Leila, and he were going to make for the Fourth. He went to get his flashlight and then he and Sheba stepped through the arched doorway and headed for the dungeon Leila had found. Sheba wasn't happy and protested with a few wheezy barks, which Jon ignored. He told her to come along and not to be a sissy. Reluctantly she trotted at his heels, her eyes fixed on the arc of light ahead.

Jon threw the light along the uneven dirt floor, over the rough walls, where several small bats clung upside down in their daytime sleep, and up to the low ceiling. Slowly he and Sheba advanced across the room. It was a good-sized one, square, but dismally lighted by the one oblong slot cut in the thick rock wall. The beam picked out an opening that was nearly blocked with rubble piled into it.

"Yes, sir, Sheba, I think I'm right and that's one of the entrances to a passage that leads outside the castle walls." Elated at his discovery, he turned back. "We'd better call this quits for today and we'd better keep it under our hats too, at least from Leila. If Aunt Agnes hears us, she may declare this out of bounds. No sense in having that happen when we've got a whole summer ahead of us."

They came out into the bright sunshine in time to hear the clock on the village church strike one. He hustled in to be ready for luncheon.

Jon was relieved when Leila began to talk about the plans for the Fourth. "Mother says she doesn't mind if we shoot off a few firecrackers to celebrate the

Fourth. We can ask Paolo to come up on the roof to help us."

Jon didn't ask what might be meant by the word "few." He had seen the expression on Leila's face, and he felt sure she deliberately meant to be vague about their plans.

As they left the dining room, Leila managed to give Jon a poke. She said softly, "Wait a sec, I want to talk to you." She maneuvered her way out on the terrace, unnoticed.

"What's on your mind?" Jon asked, unconsciously lowering his voice too.

"When can you and Paolo go shopping for our fireworks?" she asked promptly.

"We've got most of a week," Jon told her. "Why the hurry and what kind of fireworks do you want?"

"We'll want firecrackers, of course, as big and noisy as you can get. For Mother's and Amy's benefit we ought to buy some of the big sparklers, too. The fireworks we'll keep for a surprise. See if you can find out what they have in the shops and how much they cost. But please don't say a word about this to anyone. Promise, Jon?"

He promised. With sudden clarity he knew that their roles were more or less reversed. She didn't tag after him or tattle anymore, but was taking the lead. Masculine pride made Jon say: "This sounds loaded with more than black powder. It's dynamite, if you ask me. Your mother'll be furious when she hears the racket and thinks we've deceived her. If any of us blows off a finger or two, we'll all be in trouble."

Leila wrinkled her small nose at him. "How is it you've gotten to be such a fraidcat, Jonathan? I always thought you were the bravest boy in the world, and I wanted to be in on everything you did. Don't you remember?" She looked sad and added wistfully, "Maybe it was partly because you were my big cousin and partly because you were an American."

For an instant Jon was shocked at her words. Then he saw her eyes dance and he began to laugh. "Didn't your mother ever turn you over and give you a spanking, Leila? For a minute you nearly had me believing you, with that sad look and injured tone of voice. You're not going to wind me around your finger, whatever you may think, say, or do." He shook his head as he added, "Not after the Fourth, I mean."

Jon was still smiling as he and Sheba climbed the stairs to the roof. "If we're not careful, Paolo and I, and I guess you and Balou too, will be jumping through hoops for her," he told Sheba.

Jon walked over and picked up the rusted relic on his shelf and looked it over. "How are Paolo and I going to hunt for the secrets of the castle without having Leila take over?"

"Who are you talking to in there?" Paolo asked as he appeared in the open doorway.

"Only to Sheba. I'm apt to, when I've things on my mind," Jon explained, expecting Paolo to understand.

"Anything important enough for me to hear?" Paolo asked.

Jon described the scene with Leila so well that Paolo had no trouble imagining it. "What Leila wants is

action about the supplies for this Fourth of July celebration she's planning. How can you and I ever get
back control of things when you're allowed to do some
of the castle-exploring?"

Paolo agreed he would take care of Leila's request
that afternoon if he could get to the village.

Paolo made his report during his night visit to the
tower room. "I can get plenty of firecrackers—big
ones. And plenty of giant sparklers too. For fireworks
they have a few pinwheels, and some Roman candles,
but those aren't very big."

"Big enough to tie some together and set off at one
time?" Jon asked. "Are the firecrackers big enough to
put under empty tin cans and blow them sky-high?
That's fun, and noisy."

Paolo fished in his pocket. "Here's the list and what
they'll cost. I'll buy what Leila wants, but I've got an
idea we'd better keep the fireworks a secret. Some
places make you get a permit for them, and I don't
think my uncle would ask for one."

Jon and Leila gave Paolo enough money to buy a
promising supply of various explosives for their celebration. They all discreetly kept the details to themselves. The boys knew that the pinwheels were simple
to operate, but they had grander ideas about the display they wanted to make with the Roman candles.
They finally put together an ingenious arrangement
that would let them light and fire several at a time.
With plenty of lighted punk to use, they couldn't think
of anything that could possibly go wrong.

"Before I do any studying this morning, I'd like to

have some exercise," Leila announced at breakfast the morning before the Fourth. "Guess I'll ride Pinocchio up around the shrine."

"Guess?" Amy Bond asked. "If you expect to do well in your examinations, Leila, you mustn't be careless in your speech."

"Sorry, Amy, it must be that American side of me again," Leila said. "I'll be careful when I do my written work, don't fear."

She gave Jon a quick wink and held up ten fingers behind her back, to indicate she would be along in that many minutes. He and Sheba joined Paolo and Balou and they sauntered off to meet Leila on the hilltop. Balou heard Pinocchio first, and he and Sheba hustled down to meet the little donkey and his rider. In a few minutes the group had settled down for a conference. The boys leaned their backs against the wall of the shrine, while Leila sat on a hummock. Pinocchio nibbled grass nearby and the dogs sat quietly, one on either side of her.

"What's the program for tomorrow?" Leila asked, leaning over to select her inevitable blade of grass. "I know we'll have to wait until it's dark to shoot off fireworks. I've planned it so Mother and Amy will sit on the terrace and watch. That'll keep them out of our way. What I'd like to know is when we use our bangers."

Paolo and Jon had a quick conference before Jon gave Leila an answer. "Paolo thinks we'd better wait to do all our celebrating until night. He thinks too much noise during the day would bring too many questions before we want them."

Paolo interrupted to tell him another important thing. Jon continued: "His uncle's going to be away that evening so we can have our entire celebration while he's gone. I have a hunch Paolo thinks he might not approve.

"Paolo and I have collected a dozen empty tin cans that Maria had put down in the storeroom. If we put a big banger, as you call it, under one, it blows the tin up sky-high and makes a super racket."

Leila clapped her hands at the prospect. "Something tells me that Mother and Amy won't enjoy the celebration, but I'll bet the people in the village will. They'll never forget what the Fourth of July means to Americans by the time we're through."

She decided she had better get back and tackle her studying. She and Pinocchio were soon ambling down the hill and out of sight.

Paolo watched her go. "She's almost as good as another boy when it comes to planning things," he remarked.

Jon looked at him sharply. "M'mmmm, but I haven't forgotten she's my kid cousin and a girl. For instance, if anything should go wrong tomorrow, who'll take the blame? You and I will, and we won't mention it was her idea."

"But that's what you'd expect, Jon. What else could we do?" Paolo asked. "Besides, nothing'll go wrong, unless her mother gets upset when she hears the noise."

"She and Amy'll probably have kittens when they hear the racket our 'few' firecrackers will make. But the show'll be over before they can get up to stop us. Come on, we'd better begin to carry some of the stuff we've got ready up to the roof. The fat would be in the fire, if your uncle or aunt should find them here."

"Where'll we hide them up there?" Paolo inquired. "My aunt takes care of your room, my uncle looks after the garden, and your aunt goes up too sometimes."

"We can find places in my wardrobe and in the big chest. Down here someone's apt to look back of the woodpile any minute."

With stealthy care and secrecy the boys carted their supply of noisemakers and fireworks up the narrow stairs to Jon's room. They managed to hide the accumulation so no unsuspecting person would find a clue.

"Not a bad collection, if you ask me," Jon commented. "It may not be the best, but it'll do."

"What a perfect night to have your celebration, Jonathan," his aunt remarked as they finished dinner on the Fourth. "Amy and I'll sit out on the terrace and enjoy the moon and the fireflies while we wait for your display."

Amy Bond nodded. "It's unfortunate that Vittorio must miss them. I don't believe there have ever been any here before."

Jon and Leila looked quickly at each other, but neither of them made any comment. As soon as they thought it was polite, they disappeared to join Paolo on the roof.

"Poor Balou. I forgot he's afraid of thunder. He'll probably run for shelter and hide the minute we make the first noise," Paolo said, patting Balou while he tried to reassure him with his voice.

"Sheba will fade fast too, most likely," Jon said.

"She'll crawl under my bed until she feels it's safe to appear again."

Leila understood what Paolo had said from Jon's remarks and she offered to stay with the dogs and try to keep them happy.

"No, sorry, but we'll need your help, Leila," Jon said.

"Let's not waste any time. First we'll start those big sparklers in the two front towers, then set off a couple of the big crackers under the tins," Jon suggested. "The lights and the noise ought to get us some attention and an audience."

It did, for the enthusiastic shouts from the village nearby drowned out the protests from the terrace below. Balou and Sheba had disappeared at the first explosion, but the three young people went about their program without any delay.

Pinwheels spun their brightly colored lights, sparklers twinkled, firecrackers exploded noisily, and the firing of the multiple Roman candles was surprisingly spectacular.

Although shouts and the blowing of car horns encouraged the celebrators, Leila kept her ears open for complaints from her mother. Suddenly Leila warned: "Mother's furious. She's going to come up if she can make her flash work." She giggled. "That'll take time. I unscrewed the bulbs in both their torches, and hid the extras. Hurry, before she finds a candle."

Jon nodded. "Let's have our finale. Be sure your punk is glowing." He checked. "O.K. Take your places, and we'll set off the candles."

With a sputtering roar of flashing lights, the groups of Roman candles hurtled up into the clear night, each blazing trails of brilliance that surpassed all that the boys had expected.

"Oh, oh," Leila shrieked. "One of mine's in trouble. Jon, look, it's going down instead of up."

Paolo and Jon, without taking time for any pretense of translation, ran to see what was happening. They saw that Leila's group had ignited, but its thrust had carried it downward. As they peered over the wall they saw the blaze land in a tall haystack piled neatly in one of the fields below. As the Roman candles burned out, the top of the haystack blazed in its place.

The shouts of the village spectators had turned to screams. People milled about until a pair of the local police took charge and led a group of volunteers to put out the flames. Buckets of water, branches, stamping feet, and energy soon extinguished the fire and removed the threat of any more danger.

Paolo looked at Jon and sighed. He said, being careful to speak in Italian: "We're going to be in trouble any minute now. Tell your cousin to disappear. She'd better go down with her mother, and she's not to admit she knew anything about anything. Get her to hurry. I hear motorcycles coming up the drive."

Jon told her what Paolo had said. "But, Jon, it's really my fault," she protested. "I was the one who suggested it in the first place." Jon took her by the shoulders and marched her toward the stairs. Reluctantly Leila disappeared.

The boys wasted no time. They hustled down the back stairs that led to the tunnel entrance, snapped on the light, and went out to meet the visitors.

Two motorcycles swung neatly around the final

curve of the drive into the parking area. When the riders had revved the motors with a final spurt, they shut them off and stood facing both boys. Jon's heart pounded, and he felt that the silence was frightening. He didn't feel any better when he recognized one of the men as the one who had come the day he and Paolo had trespassed and gone fishing.

"Your permit, please. I wish to see your permit," the officer asked, looking first at Jon and then at Paolo.

Jon's mouth felt dry. Wild thoughts of jail and what his father would say flashed through his mind. He stole a look at Paolo and knew from the expression on his face he didn't feel much better.

Although Paolo's ready smile was missing, he did manage to shake his head and report briefly that they didn't have a permit.

"*Chè successe?*" They all turned to find Vittorio standing there. "What has happened?" he repeated, his face grave with concern.

As the tongues of the two police officers and the two boys let loose a flood of explanations, Jon knew he had never been so glad to see anyone as he was to see Vittorio.

9

⨆⨆⨆⨆⨆

Punishment Plus Plans

INSTINCTIVELY, Jonathan and Paolo edged close to each other. When Vittorio questioned the senior police officer, the boys listened politely while the man told his version of the story. It was accurate and vivid, but covered only his side on the hour's activities as he had seen it.

Jon itched to speak out, and he heard Paolo give a stifled gasp of dismay at one or two points. When the officer had finished, Vittorio asked the other officer if he had anything to add, and then swung to look squarely at the two culprits.

"This is a serious offense," he told them. "You may have to appear before our magistrate. He will probably fine you heavily for shooting off your fireworks without a permit, and for your careless use of them." He shook his head sadly. "You knew I wouldn't like this, Paolo. That's why I hadn't heard a word about it, isn't it?"

Paolo looked guilty, and Jon felt his own face hot with embarrassment. A sense of fair play made him blurt out impetuously: "But, Vittorio, we, I mean I, was the one who insisted. I urged him to help celebrate our American Fourth of July. He really didn't think you'd like it and said so. The fire was an accident, and I am sorry."

Jonathan had spoken in English before he stopped to think it might appear rude. Vittorio nodded and said in English, "I'll do my best to explain."

Jon thought Vittorio looked slight, almost frail, as he faced up to the big men in their starched white uniforms. Nevertheless he was in command of the situation when he spoke, calling both men by their names. "I realize that this isn't anything you can regard as a joke. The boys have broken regulations and caused a fire. But they are both under age and the haystack that burned was one that Nino had piled up in our lower field to cure. The boys must pay him for damages, and I ask you for permission to see that both boys are punished by me. It will work out with less trouble for everyone, and an 'international' situation is involved in this."

Jon was watching the men's faces closely, trying to see how they would react. The gleam in their eyes and the set of their jaws didn't look encouraging to him. Suddenly he was amazed to see their dark eyes light up, and a hint of smiles relax their mouths. What in the world were they thinking of that was causing them to change their minds? he wondered.

A slight sound made him turn, and he understood. Leila was smiling up at the two irate men. She spoke softly to Vittorio. "Please tell them it was actually all my idea, start to finish. I wanted to see what an American Fourth of July celebration would be like. Besides, it was my fireworks that got loose and started the fire. I'm terribly sorry."

In two languages and with gestures, Jon and Paolo tried to deny it, but it didn't matter. Leila did look like a repentant angel, Jon realized, and she was much too pretty for the gallant Italian officers to include in their official wrath. The spokesman, after a brief struggle with himself, and a short conference with the other policeman, shrugged his shoulders and then bowed to Leila.

He tried to keep his voice stern as he said to Vittorio: "We think you're right. This is an international situation which you can handle better than we." They both nodded again and turned to go. The first officer said to the boys, "Please remember, we do not want another American celebration, but everyone in the village enjoyed this one."

Vittorio told Jon he would speak to his aunt later, but for the moment he was to take his cousin into the castle. Jon heard him say to Paolo: "You are confined to the castle grounds until further notice. Another such escapade and I'll send you back to Genoa and your grandmother." They disappeared, and Paolo was looking more sober than Jon had ever seen him.

"Does Vittorio really mean that, Jon?" Leila asked in a worried voice. "It doesn't seem fair when it was my idea, not Paolo's. I'm sorry if I've gotten him into hot water."

"Perhaps it won't be as bad as it sounded," Jon said. "Maybe I'd better do some worrying on my own account. Somehow I don't think your mother's going to be too pleased with me."

Leila laughed softly, putting her finger on her lips. "She doesn't know that those policemen came, or much of anything that's happened. Act sorry when she accuses you of misleading her or me, but let me do all the talking. Promise, Jon?" She tugged at his arm.

"Listen, Leila, I'm not going to hide behind any girl's skirts," Jon told her. "I don't mind if you do the talking as long as you'll remember that." He held the door of the drawing room open for her.

"Where have you been, Leila?" her mother asked. "I sent Amy to look for you."

"I was talking to Vittorio, Mother. He had come back and I knew he'd be furious with Paolo."

Her mother interrupted. "I told you that boy Paolo was frightfully irresponsible and wild. I should not have let you all be together. He was bound to get you into trouble."

Leila shook her head. "But, Mother, none of this was his fault. It was mine, entirely mine. Ask Jon."

Jon squirmed. Before he could speak, Leila added quickly: "Of course the boys will take the blame. They'd rather lose an arm than admit it was a girl who planned today's celebration. But it was all my idea. You can blame me, the American half of me, for wanting to have a celebration on the Fourth."

"Aunt Agnes," Jon interrupted firmly, "Leila did say that she thought it would be fun, but you can blame me from there on. After all, Paolo and I are boys, and we're enough older than Leila to have some judgment. I am sorry Paolo's in trouble with his uncle."

Aunt Agnes asked quickly, concerned, "How?"

Leila told her.

"That seems a fair penalty, Leila. Since you'll be busy with your studies and your examinations, you will be confined automatically. Jonathan, I'm going to impose the same restriction on you." She looked at them and shook her head. "I hope that will allow us a few days without any further escapades."

Jon climbed thoughtfully to his tower room. "Sheba, Sheba," he called as he reached the open roof. "Sheba, all's clear. Come out now."

No Sheba appeared, and Jon looked in every possible hiding place, but she wasn't to be found. She was with Balou, he decided, although he didn't think it would be wise to go down to look for her tonight. She would surely come up soon.

Jon felt a twinge of loneliness as he leaned over the wall and looked down at the fields where hundreds of fireflies flickered and bobbed. How in the world was he going to keep busy now that they were all put on limits? Leila would be studying, and Paolo would probably have some sort of work to do.

The sound of Paolo's chirp sent his spirits soaring. He turned to see Sheba prance with awkward eagerness to greet him, wriggling nearly out of her skin with delight to be with him again. Jon scratched her back and assured her how lost he was without her.

"She and Balou were hiding together down behind the woodpile in the same spot we'd hidden our fireworks," Paolo informed him. "They wouldn't come out until I persuaded them the noise was over. Did you get in trouble with your aunt?"

She was not pleased with him, Jon acknowledged.

"I'm glad we aren't in worse trouble," Paolo said. "It was lucky for us that the haystack which burned belonged to Nino and not to the Murattis or some other family." He said he must work to pay for the loss, which meant many hours in the garden or doing other odd jobs. "We were lucky my uncle came back when he did. He told me that people around here are nervous because there's been no rain for so long. There would have been a yell for our heads if a bad fire had started."

"None of us had thought about that," Jon agreed. "My aunt has restricted me to the place, and Leila too. Of course, Leila will be stuck here anyway, cramming for her exams, and then taking them, but what will I do? Do you think your uncle will let me help you with some of your work?"

Paolo pursed his lips. "The idea of our being together wouldn't appeal to him tonight. Maybe by tomorrow he'll feel better. He said if my bones had mended enough for me to get into trouble, he thought I might as well do something useful." Paolo's nose wrinkled in disgust. "I'll have to do any one-handed chore he can find, and that means housework too."

Jon laughed. "Housework isn't for me, but if you need me outdoors, give me the word. Meantime, I'll have a go at making a floor plan of the lower levels."

"Fine," Paolo agreed. "I must go down before I'm missed. *Buona notte.*"

Next morning his aunt called Jon into the library. She spoke bluntly. "Jonathan, having you here this summer isn't as simple as your father and I had expected. Vittorio has informed me about the fire and the financial loss it has meant for Nino. Paolo must work to pay for his share, but I'm advancing what you and Leila owe. You can reimburse me from your allowance."

"Of course, Aunt Agnes. Matter of fact, I'd like to pay Paolo's share. He shouldn't be in trouble about this."

His aunt was mildly sarcastic. "That's noble of you, Jonathan, but a little late in the day. Vittorio has high standards of behavior and discipline, and I don't think it would be wise for you to interfere. You'll do well to keep busy yourself and not cause any more disturbance."

Since Jonathan couldn't think of anything to say, he stood up to go. He turned as Aunt Agnes added: "Vittorio is worried about the weather. The weather bureau warns of a severe heat wave, and if it's as bad as he fears, it won't be pleasant. You'd better find some books to read, and keep inside where it's cool."

"Books," he said to Sheba when they were alone in his room. "Sure, I like to read, but who wants to spend all summer vacation reading? Let's slip down the back way and into the moat. I'm going to start making some sketches from there."

Jon started his plan with enthusiasm, but in less than an hour he and Sheba were both aware of the stifling heat inside the moat. "Whew, it *is* hot. We'd better work on the inside and leave this outside sketching until later."

Inside he had barely roughed out the outline of the entrance when Sheba pawed up something from the floor and sniffed at it curiously. "What's that you've found?" Jon asked, stooping to pick up a short length of electric wire. "That's queer. There aren't any lights down here. Wonder where it came from." Jon shone the beam of his flashlight along the walls and found in the far outside corner the tag ends of matching wires cut close to the ceiling.

As he poked and peered, he began to find further traces of wires going far into the underground passages. It was some sort of military communication system, he decided, and carefully traced the remnants until he discovered a fuse box labeled in German.

"German soldiers were right down here where we are, Sheba!" A thrill of adventure ran though him. "That rumor about hidden treasure somewhere in the underground passages begins to look more interesting. Wish I knew who could give me some information."

Discretion kept Jon from mentioning anything about his day's activities in front of his aunt. She seemed content that he had kept out of sight and not caused her any worry. No sense in stirring things up, he felt. He was eager to talk with Paolo on the roof that night.

But when neither Paolo nor Balou appeared, Jon was disappointed. Sheba fidgeted restlessly and finally took a stroll to investigate the opening near the chimney, hidden behind the wisteria vines. She returned to sit peering into Jon's face, waiting for him to explain this desertion.

He rubbed her ears, but shook his head. "Don't expect me to tell you where they are. I've been waiting hours to have a word with Paolo myself."

They waited another hour and then turned in for the night. Jon put the three-inch piece of electric wire on the shelf beside the old spearhead.

"Poor Paolo," Leila said at breakfast next morning.

"What do you mean, 'poor Paolo'?" Jon asked, feeling a little annoyed that Leila should know anything about his friend before he did.

"It's so frightfully hot that he and Nino are getting up at dawn to work outside, and going out in the evening until it's dark. Vittorio says no man should be out in the midday heat if it isn't necessary."

Jon almost exclaimed, So that's why he didn't come up last night, but choked back the words, unspoken. He said instead, "If I had an alarm clock, I could go out and help him, poor guy."

Aunt Agnes told him that he was not to do any such thing. "Paolo's always lived in Genoa and he's used to intense heat. I'm not going to risk having you get a sunstroke. This is a definite order, Jonathan. No working with Paolo during this heat wave."

For the next few days Jon and Sheba spent many hours beneath the ancient fortress castle. He took along a flashlight, a pad of paper, and a pocketful of pencils. Patiently he paced off walls and took careful measurements where he could. It wasn't easy, for the dirt floors were rough and at uneven levels, and the passages and walls often turned abruptly because of the huge barriers of solid rock.

Jon found that it was confusing and he sometimes lost his sense of direction as he and Sheba poked into nooks and corners and followed the rambling passages into odd-sized rooms or spacious areas. Some of the latter seemed useless to him until Sheba, with her usual interest in half-hidden objects, dug up a rusty horseshoe.

"You're as useful as Sherlock Holmes in this business, old girl. This must be where they used to keep the mules and horses in the old days." Jon brushed off the dirt from the iron shoe and kept it to add to his collection.

But his interest in making his sketched plans began to wane when he realized how inaccurate they were. "They look like the pictures that first-graders make!" he exclaimed, tearing up the batch he had just finished. "You may be good company, and a good excavating detective, Sheba, but what I need is Paolo, or even Leila, if Aunt Agnes would ever let her come down here."

He had about decided to take his aunt's suggestion and spend his time reading and forget the underground exploration when Leila gave his lagging interest a boost. The talk at dinner turned again to the heat and the damage it was causing to the land which was already too dry.

Leila said: "Vittorio told me this morning that this is the very hottest weather he can remember. I was up early to have a ride on Pinocchio and he told me not to be in the sun unless I wore a hat."

Jon saw a troubled look cross his aunt's face. "Vittorio *is* worried. Everyone is concerned about the way this may end. If there's a severe storm, he's afraid it will cause a great deal of damage. It's fortunate we have the protection of the castle."

Before the dinner had ended, Leila signaled Jonathan that she wanted to see him alone. He suggested it might be cool enough to have a game of croquet, so they strolled out onto the side terrace where the game was set out.

Once alone, Leila said: "I've got news for you that'll make your hair curl. I went for a ride this morning and visited with Mr. Rafael. Guess what? Something odd and mysterious has been going on around here."

"What?" Jon asked, only half impressed.

"He's seen two strangers, who looked like Germans, snooping around recently, using binoculars. They tried to pass themselves off as bird watchers, but when he spoke to them in German, they answered him in German without stopping to think."

"Germans! Sort of 'casing the joint,' as they say at home!" Instantly Jon was alert and ready for action.

"Right! And yesterday Mr. Rafael had a letter from a rental agency inquiring about the castle. They had a client who was anxious to rent it as soon as possible and the price was of no importance. The client would bring his own staff and the present one could have a holiday." Leila paused and looked to see how Jon was reacting.

"The rental agency just happened to be a German one. Jon, don't you think this zeroes in with the story about the treasure the German soldiers either carried off or hid here in the castle?"

Jon whistled softly. "Sure, it's someone who must know where it is and wants to find it and take it away. Hey, this means it's still here."

"That's what Mr. Rafael thinks, I'm sure. He probably wants to find it himself when we go home." She leaned over to pat Sheba as she announced happily, "And I'm finished with my exams tomorrow."

"Good!" Jon's eyes shone. "What saps we'd be if we let some old bird watchers find any hidden treasure when we're on the spot ourselves."

Jon and Leila looked at each other. A broad grin spread over their faces, and they both raised their fingers to their lips. Jon nodded, "Just the three of us, you and Paolo and I."

"And the dogs," Leila added, selecting a red-handled mallet and ball. "Let's have a game. I'm too excited to go in yet."

With careful aim, she shot at the stake and Jon accepted the challenge.

10
ЛЛЛЛ

Hide and Seek

J ON'S SPIRITS were high as he and Sheba climbed up the stairs through the balmy night air. He found Paolo and Balou waiting for them.

"Back again," Paolo announced. "I've settled my account, and my aunt told my uncle I'd been so good and had worked so hard she thought I'd had punishment enough." Paolo chuckled. "She said it was too hot to get into trouble. Anyway, here I am."

"And in the nick of time," Jon said. "Listen to this and you'll see what I mean." Eagerly Jon related the conversation he and Leila had had, and showed him the wire Sheba had dug up. He saw with satisfaction that Paolo looked excited, although he made no comments.

"Well, why don't you say something? Isn't that a challenge?" Jon demanded as he realized Paolo still hadn't spoken.

"Tell me how you think I'm ever going to get permission to go down there and dig, particularly after this last escapade?" Paolo said. "And will Leila's mother allow her to go?"

It was Jon's turn to be silent. He listened thoughtfully as Paolo went on bluntly: "I suppose you'd like to keep this a secret, but we have to get shovels and picks, and if we stay down there hours on end, someone will get suspicious."

"O.K. Maybe we'll have to let your uncle in on our plans, if worse comes to worse," Jon said reluctantly. "He might be willing to help us."

"You're wrong about that, Jon. He won't, because he nearly got crushed to death in a cave-in down there right after the war. He'd been cutting and removing wires when some of the loose debris fell on him. My aunt made him promise never to work down there again."

"That probably means they won't let you or me work there either, doesn't it?" Jon asked anxiously. "Even without picks or shovels?"

Paolo shrugged his shoulders. "Not with anything more powerful than a flashlight, I suppose. And I'll bet your aunt won't let you or Leila do any digging. I can't take any unnecessary chances this time. It's not that I'm afraid, it's the thought of being sent home that stops me." Paolo's face brightened. "Say, how about Leila? Even if she is a girl, we've agreed she's smart. Maybe she could think up some kind of excuse to get us permission to go under the castle. Is there some sort of game we could play down there where it's cool?"

Jon jumped up. "That's it, Paolo. Hide-and-seek, with special rules to fit. Trust Leila to wangle permission for that. Then, after we've played a legitimate game for a couple of days, no one would notice if we began to hunt around." Jon laughed. "My maps weren't any good, but at least I know what's there. There'll be dozens of wonderful places to hide."

"Before you speak to Leila, what about this language business? Shall we keep on with two languages or shall we tell her the truth?" Paolo asked.

"Let's stick to it for a little longer. It might still be useful, and we can tell her later," Jon decided.

After Paolo and Balou had gone, Jon thought of the dungeons and the dark corners, the bats and the spiders. It would be creepy to hide or to seek in the cool, below-the-ground rooms and passages. He could hardly wait to speak to Leila in the morning.

He and Sheba met her as she came in from a visit with Pinocchio. She announced: "I just saw Paolo and Balou out for a walk. Paolo waved and yelled 'Ciao!' Do you think he's free again?"

"Yes. I saw him too, long enough to tell him your story about the German bird watchers," Jon reported.

"Isn't he keen to get started on a treasure hunt?" she asked eagerly. "Did you tell him it would be only the three of us and the dogs?"

"He's keen as mustard, but he doesn't think we have a chance to do it. He told me if we weren't careful, we'd be forbidden to go as far as the first dungeon," Jon told her. "He suggested we get you to do some advance work and see what happens."

Leila demanded to know what he meant.

"First of all, we need to have your mother on our side. To have her sympathetic. Maybe you can complain about the heat and how you need to have some fun and relaxation since you've finished with your exams," Jon suggested. "With all the space there is down where it's cool, we can have some wonderful games of hide-and-seek, the three of us and the dogs. We can make up all sorts of rules, and she'd surely approve of our playing games like that, wouldn't she?"

"Actually it's a wonderful idea, Jon. I'm sure Mother'll agree. Lucky for me this last exam is in Lit. It'll be easy. I can do it and still think about this new scheme."

Leila didn't waste any time in speaking to her mother, who thought it was a splendid idea.

Amy Bond questioned the lighting under the castle, and Mrs. Winston-Porter said there must be a hard and fast rule that they each always carry a flash.

That was easy enough to agree to, and Leila gave her mother a big hug of thanks. She looked at Jon.

"Why don't we all meet somewhere this afternoon and talk this over? We'll need to make rules for a game tomorrow."

"Good. I'll find Paolo and tell him we're going to be down in the old wine cellar at four. That suit you?" Jon asked.

He and Paolo and their two dogs were waiting in the cool, musty room when Leila joined them. The hot afternoon sun cast an oblong of light through the one small window, showing layers of dust on a long wooden table.

"This is a perfect place to meet, isn't it? You can almost smell the grapes." Leila wrinkled her nose and sniffed.

"Smells more like dust of the ages to me," Jon commented, making a running translation to cover the

talk. "Blow some of the dust off these old kegs and we can sit on them. How about using that inch of dust on the table for drawing some maps?"

After they had made a few futile whisks and given some well-directed puffs of breath to clean things up, the room was in good enough condition to serve its present purpose. A puff of dust hit Balou's nose and he sneezed in protest. Sheba found a safe corner too dark to be housecleaned.

"First, about the dogs," Jon said. "Whoever is 'it' will be alone. Each of the 'hiders' will take a dog. That'll give a 'hider' a bit of a problem and at the same time it ought to give 'it' some clues."

"Tell Leila I'll need some code words," Paolo cautioned.

When Jon repeated this, Leila nodded her head. "Let's make the rules first and the code words later. For instance, how far will our territory go? Up into the castle, or must we stay down here? There are lots of stairs going in all directions. I don't know where they go, but could we use them?"

"There's so much space here I think we'd better plan to stay below, at least for the first day. We can use the old dungeon as our starting place and for goal. I'll give you a quick tour before we play and you'll see there're dozens of places to hide," Jon said.

Little by little they drew up a set of rules for their trial games. Leila shivered when Jon mentioned spiders, and the boys laughed at her. "There are bats too, wherever there are places for them to get in and out," Jon teased.

"Tell her those openings in the dungeons were where the food was shoved in for the prisoners, and not for the view," Paolo added.

"This is going to be spooky enough without your making it worse," Jon told him. "I think we should get a whistle in case whoever is 'it' can't find the others after a certain length of time. Blowing two blasts on the whistle would mean 'allee, allee-in-free.'

"This sounds like such fun we've almost forgotten we're really here to look for clues," Jon reminded them. "We've got to make the most of the hot weather as an excuse to be down here."

Hidden treasure was not on anyone's mind when they all got set to play their first game next morning.

"I think it's only fair for me to be 'it' this first game. Leila, you take Sheba, and I'll give you and Paolo ten minutes instead of five to find your spots," Jon said. "If you can make it back to the dungeon for your goal, you're to call out so we'll know. O.K., get going."

Balou barked with anticipation as he and Paolo left for parts unknown. Sheba, aware something unusual was in the air, wriggled with enthusiasm when Leila called her. She took a long look at Jon, clearly wondering why he stayed behind, then gave up and trotted off with Leila.

The dogs were much too excited to be quiet, and their yips and whimpers gave away their hiding places. Jon caught them all easily. By noon both Balou and Sheba began to sense what the game was about and sat silently, though shivering with tension, in the various hiding places.

"Your hide-and-seek must have been a big success," Amy Bond commented at luncheon. "Even Sheba looks pleased with herself."

"We did have fun," Leila assured her. "At first the dogs gave us away, but they've caught on and can hardly wait for us to find new places to hide."

"They know where 'goal' is, too. They nearly trip us up racing for it," Jon added.

At the end of the day they held another conference, sitting on kegs in the low-ceilinged wine cellar. The rules needed to be revised, and it would be more exciting to use the many stairways as far up as the first floor.

"I've loved every minute today," Leila declared, "but when do we get going on the treasure hunt?"

Jon turned to Paolo for advice. Paolo shook his head and said they would have to have a shovel and a pickax before they could do much hunting. "Of course we can use our eyes, our flashlights, and our imaginations, but they aren't much use for digging. Tell Leila she'd better be thinking of a solution, or we'll end up getting nowhere."

Leila groaned when Jon told her what Paolo had said. "I haven't a bit or piece of an idea, Jon."

It wasn't any consolation when Paolo reported to Jon that night on the roof that his uncle said the heat record had been broken and he believed the weather was bound to change. "Whatever we do will have to be done soon. Has Leila had an inspiration yet?" he asked.

"No, nor I," Jon answered.

Before breakfast was finished the next morning, the mail arrived. Aunt Agnes handed Jon a letter. It was on official Army paper, but the handwriting was unfamiliar.

"What do you know!" Jon exclaimed as he drew out the letter and read the signature. "It's from Ryan. He reports that a memo came in from Father ordering a badminton set sent up here right away. Ryan says when it comes not to put it on the roof or the 'birds' might take off and get mixed up with the bats. That's Ryan's idea of being very funny. Where could we put it?"

Leila spoke up in a voice mild as honey. "How about that big space right under the library? You figured it must have been where animals were kept in feudal times. That would be exactly the right size, wouldn't it?"

Jon sighed. "It's the right size, but the ground is too hard to put in the stakes. We'd need some sort of tools to get it set up."

"Vittorio must have what you need," his aunt suggested. "I'll ask him to let you have the tools if you'd like."

Although they both thanked her for the idea, neither Jon nor Leila dared to look at each other. It wasn't long before they were waiting for Paolo in the wine cellar, almost bursting with their news.

"Wait till you hear," Jon burst out. "We've got it, and everything's going to be the way we wanted it after all, even a pick and shovel."

"Who did the providing?" Paolo asked, mystified.

"Well, my father, Ryan, my aunt, and your uncle all are involved," Jon answered, laughing at Paolo's expression.

"Whoever it is, I hope we'll get going soon. I've got news for you," Paolo retorted.

"What's yours?" Jon demanded, uneasy at Paolo's gloomy tone of voice.

"The walls of the entrance tunnel are soaking wet, the way they get when there's rain over the Apennines. My uncle said it's a good omen. It means we'll have rain here soon, and an end to this heat wave. Then we'll have to play outdoors."

"What's Paolo saying, Jon? Why isn't he pleased?" Leila asked.

Jon ignored her for the moment. "The set isn't here yet, so we may need a few more days. What does your uncle mean by soon? A day or a week?"

"No one knows the answer, I'm afraid. It looks as if it's going to be a race between nature and the Italian mail." Paolo laughed. "I'm not making any bets. We can't do anything about either, and I've had a new idea for our game."

11

ᒣᒲᒲᒲᒣ

A Spooky Wait

WHAT'S ON your mind, Sheba?" Jon asked sleepily. "It's too early to get up. Go away and let me sleep."

Sheba knew better. She barked and stood awkwardly on her hind legs to paw persistently at the sheets. Jon grunted with disgust and rolled over to look at the clock. He saw how late it was and heard the bell ring for breakfast.

"Wow! It is late. You're right and I'm sorry I was cross." Jon made his apologies as he rolled out of bed and gave Sheba a hasty pat. He was showered, dressed, and out of the room within five minutes.

The heat rose in smothering waves on the rooftop, and Jon and Sheba hurried to reach the comparative coolness inside the castle walls. "Today's hotter than ever," Jon grumbled. "It's enough to make anyone feel cranky."

No one talked much at breakfast. It almost seemed as if the effort to speak was more than anyone wanted to make.

Leila finally said: "I went into the entrance tunnel before breakfast. It's dripping with water on the north side. Vittorio swears it's a sure sign of rain. He expects a storm anytime."

Jon frowned at her news, feeling an irritated frustration that now nothing would work out as they had hoped. He knew that Leila was watching him, probably reading his mind.

"What's the matter, Jon?" Leila asked when they went down to meet Paolo and Balou. "You're cross as can be." Then she saw Balou standing in the doorway and stopped to stroke his smooth white head. "Why, Balou, your lovely tail's drooping and you look sad. Your master hasn't been scolding you, has he? Has the heat made him as cross as some other people around here?"

Jon protested, "I'm mad because the badminton set hasn't come yet, that's all." He repeated this to Paolo.

Paolo was disappointed. "Well, that's going to finish our excuse for bringing any tools down here for digging. My uncle says the storm will come within the next twenty-four hours. The tunnel's wet, and my aunt, who is almost never cross, snapped all our heads off this morning."

Glumly they sat on the kegs and talked, for no one had any interest or enthusiasm for racing around. Finally Paolo suggested they might as well take measurements in the old stable, and if he had any luck, maybe he could bring the tools down anyway.

Having something to do made them forget their small annoyances, and the quiet coolness began to have its soothing effect. Feeling better, they played two games of hide-and-seek with variations that Paolo made up, and by noon everyone's good humor was back to normal.

"I'm 'it' for our first game this afternoon," Leila announced when they went up for luncheon.

At the table there wasn't any word of the badminton set, and the queer tension in the air was more noticeable. Jon heard his aunt complain of a bad headache. He wasn't surprised when she sent Sheba out of the dining room because she was acting uneasy and panting noisily. Jon was relieved when the meal was over without anything worse happening.

"My goodness, but Mother is fussy today. She always is when she gets a headache. I hope she takes some of her pills and lies down until she feels better," commented Leila as she leaned over and took Sheba's big head in her hands. "Poor old girl, you didn't understand why you were banished, did you?"

Sheba's serene good nature wasn't in the least upset. She made a valiant effort to wag her corkscrew tail as she padded ahead, leading the way to join her friends. The heat might make her uncomfortable, but it didn't make her cross.

"Oh, rats!" Leila exclaimed as they gathered in the dungeon, ready to start their game. "I forgot to hunt up a new bulb for my flash. This one's nearly gone. I tell you what, you can have the usual five minutes plus the time it'll take me to change the bulb. That'll give you a chance to find some perfectly hideous hideouts."

She went off, and Balou followed Paolo through an opening to head for the seldom-used stairs leading up at the far end of the moat.

"Here, Sheba, let's see what we can find. We need a tough spot. Leila's getting too hep to all the old places." Jon shone the beam of his flashlight along the passages, through the second dungeon, and into the small room that opened out of it. He examined the stack of heavy beams that stood on end in the far corner.

"The only place in here would be behind those. If I'm strong enough to move them, we can hide behind them," he mumbled to Sheba. She watched as he struggled, and was ahead of him once he had moved them enough to make space to hide.

"Hey, where do you think you're going?" he called as Sheba disappeared. Jon wriggled cautiously after her, flashing his light to find that she had gone through a small opening, which the planks had completely hidden.

He squeezed through a rough doorframe into a narrow passage that he had never surmised existed. Sheba was moving slowly ahead. Bending low, Jon followed. They had gone but a few yards along the tunnel when a terrific crash of thunder made him jump. The crack was followed by such rolling, heavy thunder that the earth trembled.

"That's Vittorio's storm, Sheba. Sounds like sonic booms right here underground." Jon squatted down to comfort Sheba as she pressed against him, whimpering with fright.

One crack and boom of thunder followed another so closely that the underground rumblings were terrifying. Jon's curiosity about the new passage had disappeared. "You want to get out, don't you?" he muttered as Sheba indicated she hoped they could go back where they belonged. "I'm all for it. Let's turn around and get out of here."

Jon straightened up, taking care not to bump his head as he moved back. He flashed his light ahead and groaned. "No, this can't happen to us." Shocked and frightened, he realized that the heavy planks had slipped down in a tangle, making a barricade across the small opening he and Sheba had entered minutes earlier. They would be imprisoned until someone would come who could either pry the planks loose or get help.

"For once I hope Leila finds us quickly," he said, doubting whether she would ever give more than a passing glance into the little room.

As an extra-heavy rumble made the ground tremble, Jon gasped. Before his eyes, part of the wooden door-frame, rotten with age, crumbled and fell. Instantly, a trickle of dirt began to slide into the opening. Little by little it piled up, almost like sand in a giant hour-glass, he thought. He held Sheba so she wouldn't move any closer, and together they watched the end of the passage fill with dirt and stones.

"We'll have to try going out the other way, Sheba," he said soberly. "If we're lucky, we may find an opening at the other end." The light from his flash was growing noticeably dimmer, and Jon wished he had taken time to change the battery when Leila had gone to get the bulb for hers.

They inched cautiously forward, Sheba leading as Jon bent low to follow along the rough, dirty floor. "They must have dug this for midgets," Jon muttered as he ducked an inch lower to avoid hitting his head. "Maybe I'm crazy, but I think this is going downhill, too. Could it be part of that old secret escape tunnel?"

He lifted his light to peer ahead and did not see the soft spot beneath his feet. His foot slipped on some loose stones, and his ankle turned sharply, throwing Jon off balance. The flashlight flew out of his hand, and when it landed, its beam was gone completely.

Jon dropped to the ground, clutching his ankle and groaning with pain and disgust. "That ties it, Sheba. I've hurt my ankle, our flashlight's broken, and we're caught in a place no one knows about. Vittorio was right when he said it was dangerous to fool around down here."

Soon, above the rumble of the storm outside, a weird wailing howl reached the low passage where Jon and Sheba sat huddled together. "Ghosts! Paolo said they were here and that the villagers had heard them." Goose pimples stood out on Jon's arms. He didn't feel any better when Sheba put back her head and howled dismally, her stout body shivering as she did.

Again and again the eerie sound reached them, and each time Sheba answered back. Suddenly it was nearer. Sheba was still shivering, but this time Jon felt her ears lift as if she were listening to something he couldn't hear.

The ghostly noise echoed again in the low passage. "Now what?" he asked, as Sheba stopped howling and began to bark.

Jon strained his ears to listen. Suddenly he laughed with relief. "You're right, Sheba. There're no ghosts out there, it's Balou!"

Jon cupped his hands around his mouth and gave a lusty yell. "Yoo-hoo, out there." The only answer was the disheartening rattle of several stones sliding onto the loose pile already blocking the entrance.

With a sickening realization of fresh danger, Jon shook his head. "I've heard of certain sounds starting an avalanche in the snow, but I never believed it. If I can't yell, how are we ever going to let them know we're in here, Sheba?"

Sheba whimpered a plea for action, and Jon felt her move away. "No, Sheba. If we want to get out of here alive, you'd better stay here. We're in enough danger already without your going back and digging us into our graves." He made an awkward lunge to grab her, slipped, and hit his head such a crack on the rock wall that he fell, stunned and bewildered.

When his head cleared, Jon realized that Sheba had crawled toward the soft spot where he had hurt his ankle, and was starting one of her investigations. He could hear her making exploratory snufflings with her flat nose before she began to scratch. She scratched gently at first, but in a minute or two increased her efforts to a determined digging, her whole body thrown into the project. She had found something that had caught her interest.

She began to shower Jon with dirt. He was about to call her away when he heard Paolo's voice call faintly, "Jon! Jon!" and Balou bark sharply and urgently. Jon's heart pounded with hope.

He reached over and held Sheba's collar to prevent her from digging at the fallen dirt and causing more trouble. Slowly he moved along toward the entrance. Although he could hear neither voices nor barking, his courage was revived. He wanted to yell, but was afraid he might cause another landslide that would bury him and Sheba for keeps.

"Jon! Jon!"

This time he recognized Leila's voice. He puckered up his mouth and whistled.

He realized they had heard him, because ever so faintly came the reassuring answer. They whistled back. They knew where he and Sheba were. But would they be clever enough to get them out?

12

Sheba Investigates

"I CAN'T HEAR a sound. Let's hope they've gone to get help," Jon worried aloud to Sheba. He drew her close to him and gently played with her ears. "It's sort of creepy sitting here trying to hear something, when it's so black and silent."

He kept on chattering, attempting to keep up his courage. "Wonder what time it is. Probably we've been here less than half an hour, but it seems as if we'd been here a week. The storm was a doozer. Wonder how much damage was done, and if there was enough rain to save the crops."

Sheba relaxed as she listened to the flow of words, and snuggled closer to Jon to encourage him to keep talking. He did, as new fears began to worry him. "I wish I weren't afraid about what's going to happen when they try to dig us out. Maybe we'll get crushed, the way Vittorio almost was once. How can I manage to warn them to take it easy? I don't think they can hear me very well, and I don't dare yell."

Continued silence, broken only by the faint rumble of distant thunder, settled over the waiting pair. Sheba sneezed, and Jon thought he heard something scuttle along the dirt not far from him. Could it have been a rat? he wondered uneasily. Where were Paolo and Leila?

"'I know what's keeping them. They've gone to get Vittorio to help them," Jon decided with relief. Then he groaned "He's not here. I forgot that Paolo told us his uncle had taken Maria to the dentist. Perhaps the road up to the castle will have been washed out and they won't be back for hours."

Once more he thought he heard a faint sound, as though something was moving along the passage. "Sure sounds like a rat. You weren't digging in a rat-hole back there, were you, Sheba?"

Jon thought a minute and then sat up a little straighter. "Hey, I wish I knew what you were after. You weren't squealing the way you would if you were after something that's alive. But you sure were busy."

Sheba wriggled and poked her nose into his lap. "Are you trying to tell me something?" he asked. "But come to think of it, you were digging up the place where I turned my ankle. Could be that funny flat nose of yours detected something exciting." Jon shook his head at this. "No, that's too much to expect. Just the same, if we ever get out of here, I intend to come back in to take another look. I'd never be able to sleep nights until I had made sure one way or the other."

He was so pleased with this new train of thought that he could hardly wait to talk it over with the others. Wait a minute, first things first, he reminded himself. Getting out alive was the first. Jon was roused to reality when he heard Balou bark.

Voices, muffled but reassuring, drifted in, and Jon and Sheba leaned forward, listening intently. How were Leila and Paolo going to understand each other unless Paolo admitted he could speak English? He thought he could hear planks being dragged around and he was sure he heard Paolo's voice directing the activity.

It wasn't long before Jon could see through an uneven space above the pile of dirt and watch the beams of the flashlights moving about in the blackness of the adjoining room.

The planks were heavy. When they fell they must have filled much of the small room and blocked up the entrance where he and Sheba were waiting.

"You all right, Jon?" Paolo called in Italian.

"*Sì, sì,*" Jon called back, his relief so great his own voice didn't sound natural. "But take care when you do any more digging. The entrance is treacherous."

Slowly and carefully Paolo and Leila worked to move the dirt and stones away from the blocked doorway.

"Sheba and I'd like to help, but we're apt to start a cave-in," Jon called to them. "What's the matter?" he asked when Paolo muttered anxiously.

There wasn't any answer, but he could hear them prowling about.

Jon couldn't endure the suspense. "*Chè successe,* Paolo?" he asked.

With a torrent of explanation, Paolo told him that they had had to find a short piece of plank to prop up the rotten wood of the old doorframe to keep any more dirt or stones from sliding down. Leila had discovered a piece that they thought would do, and if he would be patient, they would have him out soon.

The two young people worked hard, and the pile diminished. With the broken doorframe bolstered temporarily, only an occasional bit of fresh earth was dislodged.

A good-sized hole, big enough for them to crawl through, tempted Jon to action. "Here we come," he announced to the rescuers. He let Sheba go, giving her a gentle shove ahead. Crawling along on his hands and knees, Jon went after her. His face and hands and knees were as grubby as his clothes, but his grin was broad as he looked into the blinding brilliance of the two flashlights turned down on him.

"You're hurt," Leila cried, and dropped beside him, touching his bruised ankle gently. "Got a hanky, by any chance?" she asked.

Using Jon's white handkerchief, Leila bound his ankle skillfully. "Good thing we had a course in first aid at school this year," she announced, pleased with her handiwork. "Stand up, Jon, and lean on us. We'll get you out of here between us."

"Not yet, you won't," he answered firmly. "We've got a job to do first." He laughed at the bewildered expressions on their faces. "No, I haven't lost my mind, but I might if I don't go back in there and have a good look with a flashlight."

"Take it easy and I'll tell you what happened," he said to them in two languages. Quickly but vividly he described Sheba's keen interest in the place where he had hurt his ankle. "Not much chance it's anything we're interested in, but what if it should be! I've got to find out for sure. Do either of you want to come with me?"

Leila's answer was to hand him her flashlight. Paolo's was an eager, "*Andiámo!*"

Down on his hands and knees once more, Jon led the way as he crawled cautiously through the precariously patched up doorway. Crouching low, he hobbled along the narrow passage. Leila and Paolo were close behind him, Paolo's flashlight shining a covering beam at the end.

"I feel as if I'm going downhill," Leila called.

"This may lead under the castle wall. It could be part of the escape tunnel," Paolo said.

"I had wondered about that, but your uncle would surely have known of it," Jon reminded him. He threw the bright beam from Leila's torch as far ahead as he could and said quickly, "Look there, that's the answer probably."

They could see Sheba and Balou ahead. But twenty feet beyond, the light shone on a completely closed end of the tunnel. The passage was sealed off, and from the size of the rocks and the way they were set into the ground, it looked as if they had been this way for many years.

A shower of stones flew up and hit Jon in the face. "We'd better wait where we are," he said. "If there's any excavating to be done, let that pair of eager beavers do it for us."

The trio huddled together, watching the dogs busily digging a few feet beyond them. It was clear that Sheba was the leader of the project, for Balou looked over at her for approval every few seconds.

Suddenly Paolo nudged Jon. "Look, Sheba's got something. And Balou's got a piece of something too."

They called the dogs to them and pried the newly found prizes from their reluctant jaws—shreds of cloth of some kind—moldy, rotten, and foul-smelling.

Leila's nose wrinkled as she took her turn inspecting the find. "Whew, what an unpleasant smell! You don't think they're going to dig up the body of one of the old soldiers, do you?" she shuddered. "Maybe I'll go back if you think that's what's buried here."

"That's not what you smell. It's only cloth that's been oiled. It's the oil and mold that smell," said Paolo quickly, answering her without realizing she had spoken in English and he had answered her in her own language.

Leila's eyes began to dance. She looked to see if Jonathan had noticed, but he was as intent as Paolo on the excavation that was going on. She started to say something about Paolo's English, but stopped. If this

was a game, maybe she could play at it too. What fun it could be if she kept her discovery to herself. Leila leaned forward to watch with the boys.

Sheba's stocky shoulders were nearly out of sight as she dug deeper into the hole she was making. Balou had been assigned the job of widening the area. He moved slowly along until he had torn up the surface for another two yards. From time to time, one or the other would seize, tug, and tear off more of the rotten cloth buried below the ground. It no longer interested either the dogs or the watching trio, and lay in tattered rags where the dogs tossed it.

"Must be something buried underneath all that stuff," Jon said. "Hey, look at Sheba."

Sheba had backed out of her part of the excavation. This time her jaws were empty, her flat nose almost smothered with dirt. She looked at Balou expectantly and he moved over to consult with her. Seconds later they were digging side by side.

Finally Balou yipped sharply, Sheba grunted, and both dogs backed out and turned to look at the young people.

"They want us to help them," Leila cried. "Let's see what they've found."

The dogs moved to share the scanty place. As they crowded together, Jon shone Leila's flashlight into the gaping hole and they all peeked to see what was there. Sheba whimpered and wriggled with such impatience that Jon had to hold her firmly by the collar.

"What is it?" Leila asked. "The treasure?"

Jon and Paolo leaned down and poked at the few inches of flat surface they could see. They scraped off the loose dirt and gave the lid several hard whacks with their fists.

"It looks like the top of an old chest," Jon said.

"How do we open it?" Paolo asked, this time speaking Italian.

Leila guessed what they were talking about. She said, "I'll get the ax from the woodpile."

She snatched the light from Paolo's hand and quickly went to do the errand. The boys and the dogs were still peering into the hole when she came back. Jon moved along, and Leila knelt between him and Paolo as they all dug and scraped the dirt from the top of the big box. The dogs didn't enjoy their role as spectators and moved restlessly, eager to jump in to help.

After Leila and the boys had scraped the skin off their knuckles, and their fingernails were stained and broken, the top of the buried chest was cleared. "The best thing is to break through the lid," Jon said. "We'll be here forever if we try to get at the lock. It'll be rusty, anyhow."

Jon reached for the ax, Leila held the dogs, and Paolo shone the lights so Jon could see where to swing. In three well-aimed blows Jon opened up the full length of the chest. With a few more short strokes, he made a hole big enough to get his hand inside. In a few minutes Jon and Paolo had pried off most of the top.

They gazed, awestruck, at the contents. It was Leila who reached in and pulled out a thick roll of canvas. She unrolled it carefully.

"The Lippi Madonna!" Paolo exclaimed. "It disappeared from where my uncle and the Count had hidden it. They thought it was stolen. What else is there?"

Leila brought up two more paintings. "There's something lumpy underneath," she said. "One of you boys had better take over."

Together the boys lifted out a heavy silver service and candlesticks. Although the pieces were very tarnished, the Count's family crest could clearly be seen.

"Is there anything else?" she asked.

The boys were tugging at a heavy sack tied together at the top with a leather thong. When they set it down they could all hear the clink of coins.

13

⌐⌐⌐⌐⌐

The Treasure

MONEY!" Leila exclaimed, touching the bag and feeling the small, hard coins inside.

"We'd better get out of here so we can open the sack and have a good look," Jon said, almost choking with excitement. "Leila, you take out the paintings and call the dogs so they'll be out of our way. Paolo and I'll carry out the silver and this bag."

Sheba and Balou apparently were content that their investigations were satisfactorily finished. Leila didn't have any trouble getting them to follow her through the passage, back into the small room. Once they were all safely through the passage entrance, she and the dogs sat down and waited.

Each of the boys emerged, carrying an armful of silver, which they put on a plank near Leila.

"We'll be back in a minute. The bag's so heavy we'll have to drag it out," Jon told her. He turned to follow Paolo, who was already on his knees crawling through the entrance.

Jon had barely gone under the old frame when a pebble bounced down at his heels. They all heard it distinctly, and the boys stopped moving. They could see Leila's flashlight shining after them, and were relieved when she called, "O.K."

They had barely begun to move again, when Sheba let out a bloodcurdling howl. Uncertainly, the boys stopped once more. Their feelings weren't improved when Balou, infected by Sheba's uneasiness, raised his deep voice in an equally spine-tingling noise.

"Sounds as though they'd seen the castle ghost," Paolo tried to joke.

"Sure sounds creepy. Let's hope it's the castle ghost and not ours of the near future. Hurry, Paolo," Jon urged.

Jon shone the flashlight on the bulky bag. "This is going to be tough to move. Seems as if it weighs a ton."

Patience and excitement mixed in their efforts, and without realizing it, they were chattering to each other without regard to which tongue they were using.

Leila, her ear alert for trouble, could hear them distinctly. She bit her lips to keep back her laughter. So Jon's in on this too, she thought. They think they're spoofing me, and I don't believe they realize they're speaking in English. I'll get even somehow, she vowed.

Puffing noisily, Paolo came first, with the stained bag of coins and a grubby-looking Jon scuffling along after him. As Jon came through the doorframe, he accidentally bumped the short piece of beam that propped it up.

"Jon, look out!" Leila screamed.

Jonathan rolled to one side as the weight of the shored-up dirt and stones rushed down to seal off the passageway. Suddenly there was a rumble and thud, as a heavy boulder came loose and fell to the ground. It had fallen inside the tunnel, and they were safe.

Paolo, white-faced, muttered a prayer and crossed himself devoutly. "Sheba must have sensed trouble," he told Jon. "We're lucky we aren't ghosts, after all."

Jon nodded, his own prayer of thanks given silently. His hand trembled. He reached to pull Sheba close to him and lay his cheek on her broad head.

"We all could have been in there. Who'd ever have known where we were?" Leila's voice was a whisper.

The thrill of discovering the buried treasure was forgotten as the chill of their escape gripped them.

"Jon, you don't think they'll say we were deceitful again and send me back to Genoa, do you?" Paolo asked.

Jon was dismayed. He had never stopped to think of their activities from that angle. He told Leila what was troubling Paolo. Neither boy was reassured when she clapped her hand over her mouth and gasped, "Oh!"

Before they could discuss what the grown-ups might say or what story they themselves might concoct, the dogs stirred. Balou stood up, listened, then moved out of the little room, his tail waving.

"Somebody must be coming," Jon said unhappily.

"From the way Balou acted, it's probably Vittorio," Leila added.

Paolo looked even glummer. "What'll I tell him, Jon?" he asked nervously.

"The truth," Jon told him firmly. "Hey, let's jump the gun and take the offensive. Quick, Paolo, go to meet him. Begin yelling that we need help." He turned to Leila: "You go with him and call too. Sound as if you're nearly bursting with excitement. Maybe you can even sound as if you had been about to go to find someone. Do the best you can."

In their haste they had taken both flashlights with them. Jon sat in the heavy blackness of the room, his ears straining to listen. Sheba leaned against him, her heavy breathing the only sound he could hear.

"Wish I knew what time it was, or had some idea how long we've been down here. If they've been scared about us, they'll probably be furious, and we'll be in serious trouble again," he said to her. "And Paolo might be sent back to Genoa."

Jon stopped talking to listen. He could hear women's voices, high and excited, coming nearer and nearer. He thought he heard men's voices too, and he could hear Leila talking a mile a minute.

They were close enough for him to hear his aunt say: "But, Leila, how could you have wanted to play down here? It's so dark and dirty."

Amy Bond, usually calm, said: "Look at the bats clinging all over some of the walls! Ugh!"

Jon smiled at that. Funny, he thought, I've almost forgotten the bats.

"Oh, Amy, they're harmless," Leila told her impatiently. "And, Mother, we thought it was fun, and you did agree it would be a nice cool place. Please don't be unreasonable. You won't be when you see what Sheba helped find."

Jon saw the light moving toward the opening. Leila led the procession into the disordered room. As his aunt and Amy Bond peered, wide-eyed, at the sight, Jon noticed that the raincoats they wore were dripping, and realized it must still be raining hard outside.

Balou trotted in, followed by Vittorio and a tall gray-haired man. Both men were hatless and rain-soaked, but Jon saw at once that they weren't aware of it.

They stared intently at what had been recovered from the tunnel. He saw them exchange excited glances and nods. Almost reverently Vittorio picked up one of the heavy silver candlesticks and handed it to the stranger.

"It's a piece of your family silver that we hid and couldn't find after the occupation ended, Count," he said.

Despite her feeling of alarm and irritation about Leila and Jon, Mrs. Winston-Porter turned her attention to the man whom Vittorio had addressed as "Count." Amy Bond's mouth had opened a little from sheer amazement.

Leila's quick wit prevented an awkward pause. "Mother, may I present Count Rafael Carbone, the owner of Castle Balou and our landlord?" She completed the introductions smoothly and Jon felt the tension in the crowded room evaporate, or at least be replaced by an atmosphere that was no longer threatening.

"Where did you discover these things, Jonathan?" the Count asked as he held up one of the stolen can-

vases and unrolled it almost tenderly. His eyes lighted up with the recognition of an old friend as he murmured, "The Lippi Madonna."

Jonathan launched into a short but graphic account of the afternoon's adventures. "We'd hoped to discover some of the treasure we'd heard might be hidden somewhere down here, but we never *expected* to find any." He pointed proudly at Sheba. "I don't believe we would have, either, if Sheba hadn't been here. She may have a flat nose, but it's an awfully inquisitive one."

Paolo was wriggling with impatience. When Jon finished speaking, Paolo spoke quickly, and then dragged the heavy sack of coins out for the Count to see.

"If that is my collection of ancient coins, your Sheba is worth her weight in gold," the Count exclaimed.

"Vittorio, can't you and the boys bring these treasures into the drawing room?" Mrs. Winston-Porter asked.

For the first time she noticed the odd-looking bandage on Jon's ankle. "You've injured your ankle, Jonathan," she said with quick concern. It was then that the significance of the planks strewn about on the floor, the forbidding dirt and stones piled in the splintered doorframe, and the scratched and grubby appearance of the three young people struck her forcibly.

"Were you all in *there?*" she asked Leila shakily, pointing at the closed entrance to the passage beyond.

Leila admitted that they were. She added, "Jon

and Sheba were in there alone, in the darkness, too, because their flashlight broke." She tried to reassure her mother: "Don't fret now, Mother. We're all out, safe and sound. Jonathan hurt his ankle before any treasure hunt began, and if he hadn't, probably we wouldn't have had one." She laughed. "That sounds all mixed up. I'd better explain later. Hey, Jon, what is it that Paolo says? 'Andiámo'?"

14

The Legend Goes On

EVERYONE was ready to leave the crowded little room. Jon noticed that although his aunt made suggestions, she deferred to the Count for decisions.

"We aren't going off and leave that bag of treasure, are we?" she asked him.

Count Carbone looked amused. "The treasure has been in here for many years, *Signora*. I'm sure no one will steal it in the next few minutes. Nino can come back for it."

Leila led the procession. She carried the rolled canvases. Her mother and Amy Bond followed her.

Count Carbone had a tall candlestick in each hand, and Vittorio brought the two silver pitchers. The boys were carrying the rest of the silver.

"Jon, did you hear Leila say *andiámo?* Why did she say that? She doesn't know Italian, does she?" Paolo asked suspiciously.

"Of course not. She's smart as well as a terrific mimic. And don't forget, she likes to tease. I'll bet she said that to make us wonder. She has behaved too well lately. You wait. She'll come up with some hanky-panky before long."

As Jon came up the stone stairs into the lower hall of the castle, he stopped to look out of the window. The rain was still falling, but the heavy storm was over.

They went into the drawing room and added the things they were carrying to the others already there. "See you in half an hour, Paolo, after I'm cleaned up," Jon said.

Because the storm had blown down the wires outside, Maria had lighted the candles along the walls downstairs. Later, as Jon and Sheba entered the drawing room, the candlelight cast such a soft glow over the lovely room that Jon stopped at the threshold to admire it. The silver had been set out on the long table against one of the walls, and black as it was, he felt that it looked like family treasure.

Sheba waddled over to settle down close to Balou at one side of the assembled group. Jon looked for a seat, and was pleased when Count Carbone nodded toward the bench beside him.

Leila sat nearby. "It's almost as exciting as Christmas morning with the tree, isn't it?" she whispered to Jon.

"Or like being in Ali Baba's cave," he whispered back.

They looked up expectantly as Maria hurried in and spread a wide white sheet over the Oriental rug in the middle of the room. Behind her came Nino with the sack of coins. He set it down in the center of the sheet and bowed to the Count. "*Buona fortuna,* Count Carbone," he said, and reluctantly turned to leave.

Quickly the Count told him and Maria to stay while he opened the bag. Leila asked about the paintings. He told her that he had examined all three, and that although they were mold-stained, he hoped they were not beyond restoration.

With a quick motion the Count hooked the blade of Paolo's knife into the knot of the leather thong, and with a steady pressure cut it in two. Slowly he leaned forward and toppled the bag sideways to let its contents slide out on the sheet.

Clinking against one another, gold, silver, and copper coins slithered out of the bag before the eyes of the spellbound audience. The Count and Vittorio looked at each other.

"Vittorio and I suspected the sack might contain my stolen coin collection," the Count said, "and we were right. Here it is."

"This money isn't like your Italian coins," Leila said, picking up a gold piece.

"No," the Count told her, "these are ancient ones. That's a gold florin minted in Florence. See the lily stamped on it? The word 'florin' comes from the Latin *florem,* meaning 'flower.'"

"We have a florin in England too, but it isn't gold."

The Count nodded. "Do you know why you write £, s, d, as abbreviations for your pound, shilling, and pence? In England, during medieval times, Latin was widely used as the written language. *Libra* was the Latin word for pound, so its abbreviation was £. Shilling comes from *solidus,* hence your s. And penny comes from *denarius,* which is why you write d instead of p.

Jonathan had picked up a small, insignificant coin. "This little piece can't be worth much, can it, Count Carbone?"

"That is a penny which you read about in the New Testament," the Count told him. "It wouldn't buy much in itself today, but in a collection it is priceless."

Leila noticed that after he explained about these things in English, he took time to speak to Maria and Nino in Italian. This made it impossible for her to catch Paolo, and his face looked so alert no one would guess how much English he understood.

With Vittorio and Paolo to help him, Count Carbone began to sort the various coins into gleaming stacks. Jon and Leila watched for a few minutes, then wandered over to look at the silver which was set on the long table. Leila picked up an oval bowl and turned it toward the candlelight above her head.

"Look, Jon, isn't this the head of a dog like Balou?" She pointed to the raised crest on one side and Jon bent to look.

"Of course. It must be one of Balou's ancestors. Paolo told me there had always been one named Balou ever since the first pair came. They bring luck to the castle. It's a legend."

"You mean like the one about the apes on Gibraltar?" Leila asked. "As long as the apes stay there, England will hold Gibraltar."

"That's right," he agreed. "Trouble is, Balou's the last of his line."

"Come over and see the treasure," the Count called. "I want you all to have a reward. Would you like to have a gold coin, or some modern money as soon as I sell my collection?"

Jon looked at Leila, and they both turned to look at Paolo. As if they were drawn together by a magnet, they met in a closed circle. "Why don't we say we'd like him to take any money he might give us and get a wife for Balou?" Leila suggested.

Jon said her idea was pure inspiration and reported it to Paolo, who agreed.

At their urging, Jon acted as spokesman. "Leila has thought of exactly what we'd like you to do, sir. You see, Sheba, with some help from Balou, really found your treasure. What we'd like to suggest is that you take whatever money you'd need and buy another Great Pyrenees to be a wife for Balou."

"Then you'd keep up the line, because in a year there'd be another young Balou here in the castle to keep the tradition alive," Leila added.

The idea must have pleased his aunt. She smiled up at the Count and said: "Our young people have a good idea, Count Carbone. Of course they wouldn't expect or want rewards for themselves, but I like this suggestion. I too hope you will do what they ask."

Vittorio beamed as he whispered to Maria and Nino what had been said. They quickly voiced their approval, and Maria urged the Count to agree, saying it would make them all happy.

Count Carbone looked around and then spread his hands open in a gesture of defeat. "So, you all say yes, and so it will be. Balou, my friend, you and I are the winners."

Balou got up, waved his long tail, and came over to let the Count pat him.

Suddenly Maria asked where the boys and the dogs had been when they found the Count's things. Paolo told her honestly, but without any more details than he thought wise. Jon, watching, saw Maria's eyes darken with fear and her face grow pale.

"But, Paolo, you were in the old tunnel where your uncle was nearly killed. Didn't you know where you were and how dangerous it was to go there?" she demanded sharply.

It took Paolo and Jonathan several minutes to tell her what had happened and to reassure her that it never could happen again because the tunnel entrance had caved in and was closed forever.

"It is better so," she said softly. "The Count has his treasures restored. Let any other secrets stay buried with the castle ghosts no one has ever seen." Then she said briskly: "I'll go bring in tea. It's five o'clock and time for it." The Rossi men and Balou went out with her. Only the Count remained.

After tea had been served, the Count stood up and bowed to his hostess. "My thanks for your kindness, *Signora*, and my gratitude to you young people, and to you, Sheba, for restoring my fortune." Jon blinked as he watched the Count kiss his aunt's hand, then Amy Bond's, and finally Leila's. "Nino will be in to remove these things. *Buona sera*."

Jon woke to bright, clear sunshine the next morning. He and Sheba were up early, and she was prancing with eagerness to get going before he was out of his shower. "Calm down, old girl. You can't expect to have another day like yesterday. Would you settle for a little walk before breakfast?"

Sheba clearly thought any idea was a good one as long as it meant action. She followed Jon down the twisting, narrow stairs that Paolo and Balou always used on their nightly visits. In less than five minutes they were outside the castle walls and heading for the fields.

"*Ciao!*" Paolo called from the corner of the stable, and he and Balou hastened to meet Jon and Sheba.

"What's on for today?" Jon asked.

"I don't care what we do, but whatever it is, we can't have as much fun as we did this past week," Paolo said.

"*Ciao!*"

The boys swung around to see Leila riding Pinocchio up the hill.

Her eyes sparkled with such mischief that Jon whispered a quick warning: "Watch out for her today. She's up to something."

Leila slid off Pinocchio's back and pulled his long ears gently. "He certainly is handsome, and as nice as he looks too. Isn't it too bad he can't speak or understand English?" she said to Jon. Although she had her hand on the donkey, she looked across at Paolo.

Paolo's face began to grow red, and he leaned over to pick up a stone to throw, trying to cover up his embarrassment.

The little fiend, Jon thought, she *is* up to something, just as I suspected. "And who is 'he,' Pinocchio or Paolo?" he asked.

Leila giggled, and skipped along at Pinocchio's side as she led him into the stable. Paolo and Jon exchanged wild glances.

"See what I mean?" Jon said.

Paolo nodded, chuckling in spite of himself. "This would be a good day for us to figure out plans of our own. See you right after breakfast."

At breakfast Jon thought that Leila looked suspiciously innocent. Had he better try to sound her out to learn what she might be planning to do? he wondered. He decided not to ask, and she didn't volunteer any information.

When breakfast was over, Jon and Sheba disappeared to find Paolo. After the boys had climbed the path to the top of the near slope, they sat with their backs against one of the big rocks. As they gazed off toward the clear white peaks of the marble mountains, they discussed their possible plans.

"Now what?" Jon muttered as the dogs stood up, their tails wagging and their ears alert. "Oh, no, not so soon!"

Along the trail at the crest of the slope walked Pinocchio, with Leila on his back. Her head was high, and the breeze blew her soft blond curls into little riffles.

"Hello, Jonathan. What are you and your friend with the big brown eyes going to do this morning? You're not planning to give him lessons in English, are you?" She looked off into the distance after she had delivered this cryptic remark.

"Cut it out, Leila," Jon said, trying not to laugh. "What are you up to?"

"If I told you, it wouldn't be a secret," she answered, watching closely to see his reaction.

"Humph, we've discovered all the secrets around here," he told her calmly.

"That's what you think, is it?" Leila answered, grinning at him.

"Why don't you go for a nice ride on Pinocchio?" Jon said, trying hard not to let her teasing annoy him.

"I just might. It's the right kind of day to find out if the Count's suggestion could be true." Her feet swung a little faster and her body tensed as if she and Pinocchio might fly off into space whenever she gave the signal.

Paolo swung around and started to ask her a question.

"What did you want to know, Paolo?" she asked him directly. "I'm sorry I can't speak Italian, so we might as well use English."

Jon's mouth flew open with surprise. It wasn't until he heard Paolo's shout of laughter that he recovered enough to laugh too.

"How did you find out, Leila? When did we slip up?" he asked when he had caught his breath.

"That, Cousin Jonathan, is another one of my secrets," she told him. "Now, are you two interested in joining me to hunt for the other end of the tunnel?"

She turned Pinocchio around toward the valley. "Of course I'll need the dogs. We're going to have some digging to do." As she started Pinocchio moving, she looked over her shoulder at the boys. "Want to come?" she asked.

"Sure," they shouted together.

With two giant steps Paolo was on her left and Jon on her right. They forgot that Leila was only a girl as they set out, a team of explorers, with Balou and Sheba bringing up the rear.

Italian Phrases

Andiámo!	Let's go
Arrivederci!	See you later
Avanti!	Come in
Buon giorno	Good morning
Buona fortuna	Good luck
Buona notte	Good night
Buona sera	Good evening (afternoon)
Chè successe?	What has happened?
Ciao!	familiar form of "hello"
Divieto di pesca	Fishing forbidden
sì	yes
signora	Mrs.
un poco	a little
va bene	very good—O.K.